"*Adam.*"

His eyes gleamed down at Sunny as he continued, "After the way you kissed me, I think you'd better call me Adam."

"You kissed me, Mr. Treherne."

"A kiss like that requires two. Call me Adam."

"I admit I, uh, did participate somewhat in the exercise." She ignored his snort. "But I don't intend to repeat the error, and since we will never see each other again I see no reason to call you anything at all." She picked up her glasses and resettled them firmly on her face.

"Good night, Mr. Treherne."

"Adam." He reached for the doorknob. "I'll see you in the morning."

Dear Reader,

It's raining men! Welcome to Harlequin Romance's exciting miniseries, **Holding Out for a Hero.** Every month for a whole year we'll be bringing you some of the world's most eligible bachelors. They're handsome, they're charming but, best of all, they're single! And as twelve lucky women are about to discover, it's not finding Mr. Right that's the problem—it's holding on to him!

This month it's the turn of popular author Jeanne Allan with *Moving In With Adam* (#3408). In the coming months look out for books with our **Holding Out for a Hero** flash by some of Harlequin Romance's best-loved authors: Betty Neels, Lucy Gordon and Rebecca Winters. Next month it's the turn of Leigh Michaels with *The Daddy Trap.*

This is one series you don't want to miss!

With best wishes,

The Editors
Harlequin Romance

Some men are worth waiting for!

Moving In With Adam
Jeanne Allan

Harlequin Books

TORONTO • NEW YORK • LONDON
AMSTERDAM • PARIS • SYDNEY • HAMBURG
STOCKHOLM • ATHENS • TOKYO • MILAN
MADRID • WARSAW • BUDAPEST • AUCKLAND

ISBN 0-373-03408-3

MOVING IN WITH ADAM

First North American Publication 1996.

Copyright © 1996 by Jeanne Allan.

This edition published by arrangement with Harlequin Books S.A.

® and TM are trademarks of the publisher. Trademarks indicated with
® are registered in the United States Patent and Trademark Office, the
Canadian Trade Marks Office and in other countries.

Printed in U.S.A.

CHAPTER ONE

WHY did things like this always happen to her? Of all the places for a stupid nail to stick up... An experimental move confirmed the situation was as hopeless as it was ludicrous. The nail had securely skewered her jeans to the window frame.

"Don't stop there. Come all the way in."

The disembodied voice springing from the darkness sent Sunny's heart leaping to her throat. "Who's there?" she asked in alarm, blinking as light flooded the room. A huge, dark-haired man stared ominously at her from the other side of Blythe's kitchen. Sunny's mouth went dry. "Who are you?" she croaked. "What are you doing in Blythe's house?"

The man's clothing slowly registered on her brain. Black sweatpants, a black sweatshirt and black running shoes. He needed a shave. It didn't take a genius to figure out the man was a criminal. A criminal she'd interrupted in the middle of burgling her sister's vacation house. Fighting waves of fear that threatened to engulf her, Sunny clamped her fingers on the wooden windowsill.

"I'll ask the questions," the burglar said coldly. "Get in here."

"I can't," Sunny blurted. "I'm stuck on a nail." Instantly she realized she'd stupidly informed a hardened criminal she was trapped and at his mercy. Don't let him know you're scared, she told herself. She had to try and bluff her way out of this mess. "I'm not answering any questions until you tell me who you are."

His lips quirked at her ignominious predicament. "You're pretty cocky for a punk who's nailed to the window." He strolled across the floor to rest a hip on the wooden kitchen table, his gaze never leaving her face.

Sunny couldn't decide whether his amusement at her situation meant more or less danger to her. Deciding she'd rather not know, surreptitiously she renewed her efforts to free herself from the traitorous nail. To no avail. She was firmly caught. There'd be no escape that way; she'd have to rely on her wits. What she had left of them. Plastering what was undoubtedly the world's sickliest smile on her face, Sunny said, "You know what? I'll bet I'm in the wrong house."

"Honey, you're assuredly in the wrong house."

Under the circumstances, overlooking the sarcastically offensive endearment seemed prudent. "Yes, well, as soon as I get loose, I'll be gone." A brilliant idea struck her. If she pretended she thought he lived in the house, he'd never suspect she'd guessed his larcenous intentions. "I'm sorry I bothered you. In your own house," she added.

He lifted a dark, mocking eyebrow. "A minute ago you said it was Blythe's house." Leisurely he shifted his hip from the table, rose to his full height and took a step in her direction.

"I obviously made a mistake," she said hastily. Not that she expected for a second to convince him of that. Burglars knew whose house they were burgling.

"You made a mistake all right, honey, thinking this house would be easy pickings for a female urchin such as yourself." Moving toward her until he stood only a few feet away, the thief inspected her as if she were a particularly nasty species of insect.

Sunny knew exactly what he was seeing. Knowing the day's drive would be long, she hadn't inserted her contact lenses and dark-rimmed glasses framed her eyes. A frayed, brown knit cap failed to hide dark braids, and Grumps's faded jacket was stained from years of gardening. But even if she did look like something the cat dragged in, it wasn't this criminal's place to sit in contemptuous judgment of her. He was the one who had no business being in Blythe's house.

Now, however, was hardly the time to gird herself in righteous indignation. First she had to free herself and get to the police. Then this overage juvenile delinquent would get his comeuppance. Her heartbeat speeded up to triple time as he moved closer and stopped directly in front of her. A head taller than her five feet three inches, he loomed menacingly over her. She forced herself to look up at him, her throat stretched and raw with the effort to contain the screams she felt rising there. "If you'll just help me get loose," she said desperately, "we can both go about our business."

He pressed his palm against her throat, his fingers encircling her neck, and stared thoughtfully down into her upturned face. "Hasn't anyone told you what happens to little girls who run around after dark playing dangerous games?"

She swallowed hard. "I'm not—" His mouth cut off her denial. A hard mouth, pressing a punishing kiss against her lips. She tried to break free, but his hands grabbed her braids and held her captive.

"A little girl like you should be worried about a bogeyman dragging you off to his bed."

Before Sunny could protest his monstrous conduct, his mouth was once again pressed against hers. Only this time his lips were soft and persuasive. Heat from his mouth flashed through her. Fear and anger combined to give her strength, and Sunny thrust all her weight against his chest. She'd have had more success moving the Rock of Gibraltar.

He raised his head, looking down at her with hooded eyes. "Hopefully that will teach you to stay home at night. The dark holds all kinds of dangers for little girls like you."

"I'm twenty-five," she spat before she realized how inappropriate the remark was.

His teeth flashed white in a forest of black stubble. "Then you're too old and too inept to begin a life of crime."

Amusement only slightly softened the harsh, cynical face. Black hair, almost blue under the kitchen lights, was brushed with premature gray on the temples. Mocking laughter lurked deep within black-brown eyes. The dimple in the dark, rough chin was ridiculously out of place on a man so overwhelmingly masculine.

"If you're through taking inventory," he said dryly, "perhaps we could get back to the subject at hand."

Sunny's cheeks flamed with embarrassment, but she wasn't about to let this gargantuan throwback from the Stone Age know she was terrified. Especially since it appeared he was so arrogant it hadn't occurred to him she might pose a threat. Why should it? She didn't see a weapon, but it didn't take a genius to realize it wasn't fat sculpting his body. He could overpower her in seconds, especially nailed as she was to the window.

She gave him a persuasive smile. "I'd appreciate it if you could help me."

His answering smile parodied hers. "I'm still waiting to hear who you are."

"It doesn't matter. You might say we're just two ships passing in the night. So to speak," she added lamely.

"I'll decide what matters. Tell me who you are," his every pore reeked with menace, "and why you're breaking into the Reeces' house?"

"Sunny Taite," she said instantly. Craven and stupid, that's what she was. Any ignoramus knew enough to give a false name. Yeah, and ignoramuses probably didn't have escapees from Alcatraz scowling dangerously at them. "And I'm not breaking in. I'm Blythe Reece's sister."

"Blythe Reece's sister," he repeated skeptically. Reaching for her again, he pulled her back against his chest and felt beneath her for the guilty nail. "Are only your jeans caught?" At her nod, he gave a quick tug and the sound of rending fabric ripped through the room before he set Sunny down on the kitchen floor.

"Thank you." Holding a hand behind her over the damage, Sunny backed unsteadily away from him toward the back door. "I'll leave now. Thanks again."

Iron fingers closed about her arm. "You wanted in. You're in. Why hurry away, Blythe Reece's sister?"

His tone of voice made it clear he didn't believe her. Did burglars worry about competition? No honor among thieves and all that . . . ? She'd better convince him she was who she was. Then she'd figure out how to escape.

"I'm Blythe's sister, and—" She glanced wildly around. "I can prove it." Sunny nodded in the direction of the front of the house. "In there. Photographs. Me with Blythe, me with Mom, and Blythe and me with the boys."

An imperious hand in the small of her back propelled her across the kitchen toward the sitting area. The burglar snapped on another light and in turn inspected the photographs and Sunny's countenance, all the while maintaining his firm grip on her arm. Forced to stand much too close to him, Sunny was intensely aware of him, and she wasn't real crazy about the sneaking suspicion that tingling nerve endings and a heightened awareness of blood coursing through her veins had less to do with fear and more to do with the burglar's devastating masculinity.

She was clearly a deranged idiot. The man was a brute and a thief. No woman in charge of her mental faculties could possibly think of him in terms of sexual attraction. No wonder she'd come close to flunking chemistry in high school.

"I guess you are who you claim to be." He slowly raked her body with a cool gaze. "So you're a sister of the sophisticated Denver socialite, Blythe Reece." One corner of his mouth curved upward. "I'd never have believed any sister of hers would be caught dead dressed as you are."

Sunny stiffened. "I'm Blythe's sister, not her clone." She shook loose of his grip. "And what makes you the expert on Blythe?" He didn't need to answer because the answer was obvious. "You snooped through her dresser drawers. That's repulsive."

The sudden narrowing of his eyes reminded her that offending this man could be dangerous. In the large room, a clock steadily ticked off the minutes, the innocent sound somehow ominous. Sunny attempted an ingratiating smile. "Never mind. Let's both just forget about this whole little incident."

"Blythe Reece being your sister doesn't explain why you were entering her house through a back window." He eyed her thoughtfully. "Or explain why you turned off your lights as you drove up the street and why you killed the car engine and coasted into the driveway."

"There were deer in the yard and I didn't want to spook them."

"I didn't see any deer."

"They ran away."

"And I suppose a bear was standing beside the front door making it necessary for you to come in through a window."

A burglar was bad enough, but a sarcastic one was beyond bearing. The nerve of him grilling her when he was the common criminal. "I'm not the burglar," she flashed. "I'm not the one dressed in black from head to toe." As her words echoed beneath the tall ceiling, Sunny's stomach heaved. She was certainly winning bonus points for stupidity tonight. Why didn't she just invite him to shoot her?

He stared blankly at her before his lips slanted wickedly. "Had I realized I would be entertaining, I would have worn a tuxedo." His eyes glinted with silent laughter.

Once again Sunny's brain insisted on sending mixed messages. One side told her to run; the other noticed how darned attractive laughing brown eyes could be.

Why hadn't her mother told her insanity ran in the family?

"Well, it's been nice meeting you." She sidled toward the door. "On second thought, I think I'll just spend the night in Denver with Blythe." The heck she'd go to Denver. She'd drive straight to the police station. This man was probably the slickest thief who ever lifted a pair of diamond earrings. She took a couple more furtive steps. The door wasn't that far away. Maybe if she ran fast...

Reaching lazily out, he wrapped his large hand around her wrist and plucked her back. "You haven't satisfied my curiosity as to why you were coming through the window."

"What difference does it make? Why are you so obsessed with how I get into my sister's house? I'm not interrogating you, and you're the one in the middle of stealing whatever it is you steal.''

Great going, Sunny, she mentally fumed. The last thing she needed to do was irritate someone who undoubtedly headed the FBI's Most Wanted list. Don't show fear, she reminded herself.

"Let go of my arm. You can't scare me. Everyone knows burglars avoid murder and mayhem because if they hurt anyone while committing a crime, the penalties when they are caught are more severe.''

A look of secretive mirth flashed across his face. "If they are caught.'' He propped a shoulder against the wall. His viselike hand holding her wrist, he ran the fingers of his other hand up and down her arm. "I don't mind' occasional mayhem—'' he played aimlessly with her fingers "—if it gets me what I want. And right now I want to know why you were coming through that window.''

Sunny's fledgling confidence that he wouldn't hurt her instantly evaporated. Surely he wasn't thinking of breaking her fingers. That happened in the movies, not in her sister's vacation house in Estes Park, Colorado. Sunny couldn't decide if she was about to giggle out of nervousness, sheer terror, or because the whole situation was so ludicrous. "Blythe loaned me the use of her house.''

"But not the use of her front door,'' he said, the words coated with heavy sarcasm.

"She told me to come through the window...'' His unblinking stare further unnerved her. "Why are you looking at me like that?''

"I find it hard to believe Mrs. Reece would instruct her sister to come through the window.'' He rubbed his finger over her knuckle.

Tempted as she was to spit in his eye, the look on his face, not to mention his size and the way he was holding her middle finger, persuaded her it would be far wiser to explain. "Blythe couldn't find the key." Improvising rapidly, Sunny widened her eyes to convey sincerity. "And she told me if I jiggled the window lock it would come undone. Daniel and David, my nephews, do it all the time."

"I'm sure they do. And I'm equally sure their mother knows nothing of the broken lock."

"Of course she does. How many times do I have to tell you...?" She read the answer on his face. "Oh, all right. Blythe doesn't know I'm here. I mean, it's OK. She offered me the use of her place. I didn't tell her I was coming because I didn't want to stop in Denver to pick up the key. Blythe would have a fit if I didn't stay there, and I didn't want to stay. I was going to call her as soon as I got in."

"So your sister has no idea you're here."

Appalled by her own stupidity, Sunny opened her mouth but no words came out. The knowing grin on his face told her he was having no trouble reading her thoughts. She managed a feeble smile.

"Well, not exactly, that is, I left a message on her answering machine. She'll know by now I'm here. And she'll be calling any minute to check on me." The cynical disbelief on his face spurred her on. "She's my older sister. You know how they are. Well, maybe you don't, because maybe you don't even have an older sister. I mean, I really don't know anything about you, do I? And naturally I have no idea where you live and I probably couldn't even describe you to the police..."

She faltered momentarily. "I don't know what made me say that about the police, because of course I have no intention of calling them, because after all, you were nice enough to help me, and, uh, friends don't, uh, rat on friends, do they?" she finished in a rush, not liking the growing amusement in his dark eyes.

Suddenly the emotions of the long day's incredible events, combined with exhaustion, sapped the strength from Sunny's legs. She slumped to her knees. Only the thief's grip prevented her from sprawling full-length on the floor. Humiliating tears burned her eyes, and she wiped ineffectually at the moisture.

He stooped down beside her, a dark frown on his face. "What's the matter? Instead of playing cute little games with me..." He roughly rubbed a tear from her cheek. "Why didn't you tell me you injured yourself climbing through the window?"

Sunny tried to fend off the hands probing along her legs and thighs. "Stop it. I'm not hurt."

He sat back on his haunches steadily scrutinizing her face. "How far did you drive today?"

She closed her eyes under his intense gaze. "Too far." Sensing his impatience, she added wearily, "From Omaha."

"Have you been ill?"

The angry undercurrent to his voice told her she'd better answer. "I had the flu."

He bit off an expletive. "When did you last eat?"

Sunny dragged open her eyelids. "I don't know. I had a hamburger somewhere for lunch. I intended to eat dinner as soon as I got here." Perverseness made her add, "Unfortunately, I got distracted."

He snorted. "Come sit in the kitchen where I can keep an eye on you." Giving her no opportunity to argue, he hauled her up from the floor and back into the kitchen where he propped her on a wooden chair. Opening and slamming cupboard doors, he said over his shoulder, "It looks like you'll have to make do with canned soup. Unless you brought some supplies with you."

"They have grocery stores in Estes Park," she said defensively. "And I can fix my own soup." She started to stand.

He pushed her none too gently back down. "I said sit."

"Don't tell me you're one of those burglars who cooks in every house he robs."

He took a mug of soup from the microwave and set it in front of her. "What do you do? Spend your days reading the tabloids? I've never heard such a hodge-podge of nonsense about burglars."

The soup warmed all the way down, and Sunny could feel the strength flowing back into her muscles. "I'm sure my knowledge doesn't begin to compare with your actual experience. You're probably known to every policeman in a four-state area."

"I don't know about four states." His eyes brimmed with mirth. "But I know my share of policemen." Tossing a box of crackers on the table, he sat down across from her. "Not for the reason you've dreamed up, however. Before you decide to go dashing off into the night in search of rescue, let me assure you I'm not a burglar, and I'm not wanted by the police."

"Right." Sunny bit into a cracker. It was amazing how a little food gave one courage. "You just happened to be standing in the middle of Blythe's empty, dark house when I arrived."

"Since you appear to be so knowledgable about larcenous behavior, you ought to know no burglar in his right mind would have stuck around for conversation once he heard you coming through the window."

"It's too bad you didn't hear me, isn't it?"

He grinned. "Honey, you made more noise coming through that window than a Sherman tank."

"Well, excuse me for not having your expertise when it comes to breaking and entering." She chewed thoughtfully. "Did you luck into an unlocked door or window? Or are you one of those burglars who never met a lock he couldn't pick?"

"Actually..." He reached into his pocket and pulled out a house key, dangling it over the table. "I came in the front door."

"Are you telling me that key is to the Reeces' front door? Where did you get it?" She attempted to snatch the key.

He held it out of her reach. "From Dillon Reece."

"I don't believe you. Why would he give you the key?"

"To keep an eye on his house."

He might have mentioned earlier that he was a security guard, Sunny thought indignantly. "Well, now that you've done your bit to stem the rising tide of crime, you can give me the house key and run along home."

He stuck the key back in his pocket. "I could." He gave her a considering look. "You claim to be twenty-five," he emphasized the number, "but you look like a teenager. I'm still a little concerned about your method of egress here. Sure you're not a runaway? Do your parents know where you are?"

Sunny slammed the empty soup mug on the table. Digging in her jacket pocket, she extracted her billfold and threw it at him. "Check my driver's license."

He flipped through the contents. "Sonia Taite?"

"I was named after a great-aunt. Everyone calls me Sunny." She took back her wallet. "Are you satisfied now? I'm twenty-five years old and I haven't run away from home." At least, not the way he thought.

"Altering a birth date on a driver's license is the oldest trick in the world."

"You are absolutely the most suspicious person I've ever met in my life. Do you see spies under your bed and murderers around every corner? This is Estes Park, Colorado. Small town, U.S.A. Not exactly the crime capital of the world."

He ignored her outburst. "How ill have you been? Are you still under a doctor's care?"

"All I had was a slight case of the flu." Shoving back her chair, she stood up. "Do you think we can cut short the inquisition? I've had a long day."

"Maybe you ought to spend the night at my place."

"I'm not going anywhere near your place, and if you try and drag me into your bedroom, I'll scream so loudly, Blythe will hear me clear down in Denver."

"What an inventive mind you have. Believe me, you have nothing to worry about along those lines. I happen to be rather fastidious about whom I invite into my bed." In an abrupt change of subject, he said, "Give me your car keys."

Sunny ground her teeth. "No, I am not going to give you my car keys. I am not going to spend the night at your place. I am not going to put up with you for one more second. I don't care if you're a member of the CIA, if you don't go away this very second, I am going to have an absolute, screaming fit."

He stared at her a long moment, his forehead wrinkled in thought. "You still look awfully pale, but all right," he finally said. "You can stay here tonight."

"How very kind and gracious of you to allow me to stay in my own sister's house. Now, go away. You don't even need to bother to apologize for your outrageous conduct."

"I have no intention of apologizing for being a conscientious neighbor."

"Neighbor?"

He paused at the back door. "I have the place next door."

Sunny shook her head. "I happen to know all about their next door neighbor, and you're not him. He's a big, ugly, dark-browed brute, a rude, surly hermit who hates women and children. To say he's a crabby curmudgeon would be flattering him. He's bad-tempered—" At the strange look on his face, she stopped midsentence and clapped a hand over her mouth. "Oh, my goodness." A weak giggle escaped her. "You are the neighbor."

"Adam Traherne." He sketched a mocking salute. "As delightful as our visit has been, I'll say good-night."

The door closed behind him with a loud snap. Sunny stared blankly at the door. She was finally alone, but her mind refused to operate. The task of washing the few dishes Adam Traherne had used seemed monumental. Driving five hundred miles in one day by herself had been crazy. Overwhelming fatigue claimed her body. Folding her arms on the table to prop herself up, Sunny decided, in her present condition, coping with Blythe was out of the question.

Blythe would demand answers Sunny didn't have. All she knew was this morning she'd awakened in Omaha, Nebraska, trembling from the aftermath of a nightmare in which a dark, heavy cloak had floated slowly, inexorably down to completely smother her. Chilled, her heart thudding, she'd wanted nothing more than to burrow deeply beneath her blankets and never come out.

Of course Grumps had had a great deal to say about that. Not even the cold, depressing sound of rain splattering against the windows had changed his mind. The only battle she'd won was driving to Colorado instead of flying. Even Grumps had conceded she'd need her car if she wasn't to be a prisoner of Blythe's well-meaning, but suffocating, older-sister solicitousness.

An hour out of Omaha on Interstate 80, her car headed west, the idea had come to Sunny. She'd go directly to the empty house in Estes Park. No friends or relatives. No phone. No letters. No Blythe with the inevitable custard pudding or chicken soup. Just peace and solitude.

Then had come the nail. And Adam Traherne. Laying her head on her crossed forearms, Sunny surrendered to semihysterical giggles. Adam Traherne. Blythe's ranting and raving about the man who'd recently built a vacation home next to the Reeces' mountain home had dominated Blythe's long-distance phone calls to her younger sister ever since the man had moved in.

His first sin had been refusing an invitation to one of Blythe's summer barbecues. His second was complaining about the Reece sons. Blythe might be every inch the elegant sophisticated socialite Adam Traherne had described, but that didn't mean she wasn't a tigress when it came to her three boys. She and Adam Traherne had clashed over teenage behavior more than once.

According to Blythe, the man was totally unreasonable when it came to balls accidentally bouncing against the side of his house, and obviously he'd forgotten his youth, the way he carried on about noise. The kids and the radios were in her yard, Blythe had emphasized repeatedly in her phone conversations with Sunny. Sunny closed her eyes. When Blythe was in a temper, she wouldn't see an elephant charging her. Which is probably why she hadn't noticed the dimple in Adam Traherne's chin.

* * *

Sunny spent an exhausted, restless night anticipating a phone call which never came. She'd been positive Adam Traherne would run straight to his phone to call up the Reeces to report on Sunny's presence in their vacation home. Of course, Blythe not phoning didn't necessarily mean Adam Traherne hadn't contacted her. Blythe was quite capable of being too furious with her baby sister to speak to her. She wouldn't be happy Sunny had thwarted her plans. The suggestion that Sunny come to Colorado had been Blythe's. A change of scene would be the best medicine, she'd said, offering the Reeces' summer home in Estes Park, a small resort community at the gates of Rocky Mountain National Park. Grumps had leapt at the invitation.

Sunny was well aware her older sister had offered the mountain vacation home with every intention of keeping Sunny in Denver. And she suspected Grumps thought so, too, or he wouldn't have given in on the matter of her driving. Two days, he'd insisted. She was to take two days to make the trip. Grumps's and Blythe's belief that Sunny was spending one night enroute in a motel is what had enabled her to circumvent their plans.

Now Sunny had to call Blythe and confess what she'd done. No doubt Blythe had figured out the exact minute when Sunny should be driving into the driveway of the Reeces' Denver home. When Sunny didn't, Blythe was fully capable of setting every law enforcement agency between Omaha and Denver on Sunny's trail.

Taking a deep breath, Sunny picked up the phone. Thirty minutes later she hung up, Blythe's recriminations and advice ringing in her ear. Blythe was not pleased Sunny had slipped past Denver without stopping. Blythe didn't believe in indulging illness. Fresh air, getting out, keeping busy were Blythe's remedies. Sunny's throat choked her as she studied hands held out in front of her.

Hands that felt more like smashing and slashing in anger
than painting dainty flowers or creating fairy tales.

Standing in the back of the house, in the huge L-
shaped room that served as kitchen, dining area and
sitting room, Sunny rubbed her chilled arms. A ceiling
braced with heavy beams soared high above her. On clear
days the huge windows draped with a faded floral print
framed a breathtaking view of Longs Peak. Today, late
in October, the foul weather lashed at the glass panes
while low clouds and spitting snow shrouded the
mountain peaks.

Shivering, Sunny grabbed a worn quilt tossed over one
of the heavy Mission oak chairs and draped it over her
shoulders. Coming here had been a mistake. If she'd
had to go somewhere, a cruise would have been better.
Pampered passengers lolling around the decks, their
every whim instantly met. Pure, unadulterated self-
indulgence. Handsome ship officers dancing attendance
on unattached women. Her mouth turned down. With
her luck, every male on board would be accompanied
by a wife or over eighty or a gigolo looking for a heiress.

Or else an anachronistic throwback to Medieval times
such as the busybody next door. For all his protestations
of watching a neighbor's house, not such a busybody
that he'd called Blythe. Which made one wonder. Maybe
he didn't want Blythe to know he had a key to her house.
He claimed Dillon had given it to him, but saying something didn't make it true. She ought to ask Blythe, but
her sister was bound to react to the question in some
way that Sunny was simply too drained to deal with.
Besides, there could be no earthly reason for Adam
Traherne to steal his neighbor's house key. Obviously
Dillon had given the key to his neighbor as a security
measure. And knowing his wife's dislike of the man,

Dillon had deliberately neglected to mention that fact to Blythe.

Blythe only thought she knew everything. She hadn't known about the faulty latch. Protecting her nephews, Sunny claimed she'd discovered it on her previous visit and promised to have it fixed as soon as possible. Anything to get Blythe off the topic before her sisterly radar picked up the slightest suggestion that Sunny wasn't being entirely forthcoming on the subject of her entry into the house. If Blythe knew her villainous neighbor had kissed her little sister, she'd rush to Estes and drag Sunny back to Denver.

Memories of a dark, brooding face leaning down toward her invaded Sunny's thoughts, as they had, with disturbing regularity, throughout the morning. Only because the man gave her the creeps. Any chills he sent up and down her backbone were from distaste. Dark brooding heroes held no appeal. Adam Traherne was more suited to play the role of a mad killer or a gangster on the lam. A black, double-breasted, pin-striped suit with a black fedora pulled low over his brow and an Uzi resting on his hips would suit him to perfection.

From habit, she'd brought her drawing materials, and they lay on the table where she'd tossed them after unpacking her car. Sitting down, Sunny stared at them. Hesitantly she reached for the pad and a pencil. The pencil felt awkward in her hand. There was a small thud as it fell back on the table. The fingers on her right hand slowly flexed, and she groped toward the pencil. The sketch pad was open to a blank page. Slowly Sunny raised the pencil. A black line appeared on the paper.

The dimple in Adam Traherne's chin begged for caricature, but she resisted, barely sketching it in. More interesting was the malevolent air that could be suggested by piercing black eyes and dark stubble. An hour later

Sunny sat back and stretched tight muscles, at the same time appraising the drawing propped on the table. If this man wasn't wanted by the FBI, the CIA, and Interpol, he should be. The piercing summons of the front door bell interrupted her.

A middle-aged man standing on the doorstep stuck out his hand. "Afternoon. Jeb from the hardware store. I'm here about the window."

"Window?"

"Man said the lock was broken and he wanted it fixed."

"Oh. It's this way." Sunny stood back, allowing the repairman to enter. Blythe must have called Dillon the minute Sunny hung up. "In the kitchen."

Jeb was garrulous but efficient, and he soon departed, leaving behind a securely locked window. Blythe had told Sunny where to find an extra key, thankfully sparing her the danger of another run-in with any neighbor. If Sunny never saw a certain hulking brute again, she'd be ecstatic. An opinion, she was absolutely positive, that the hulking brute shared.

CHAPTER TWO

ADAM Traherne rapped once on the back door as he walked uninvited into the kitchen. "You ought to lock your doors."

"Why bother? You have a key."

Ignoring her caustic rejoinder, he walked over to the newly installed latch. "There's no point in paying for new locks if you plan to leave your doors wide open."

"You must camp beside your window spying on this house night and day. How did you know that man was here to fix the window? His panel truck was unmarked."

He rattled the window, but the lock held. "When I called the hardware store, I told them I wanted it repaired today."

"You called..." She stared at him in disbelief. "He said a man called. I thought he meant Dillon. Do you ever mind your own business?"

"I didn't think—" he continued to test the lock "—a woman brainless enough to jump into a car, without food, and drive across an entire state to break into a empty house was the kind of woman likely to take care of a broken lock. And that is my business. Dillon Reece and I have an agreement to watch out for each other's home."

"Now that I'm here, you can hang up your spyglass. I'm perfectly capable of acting as caretaker." She decided to graciously ignore the mocking look he sent her way. "And if you came to apologize for your crude behavior last night, just leaving me alone will suffice."

"Crude behavior?" A maddening smile crawled across his face. "Don't tell me you're referring to the kiss?"

"Of course I'm referring to that disgusting kiss."

"Funny thing about that kiss. The whole idea was to scare a young girl into considering the possible consequences of her dangerous behavior. I should have realized you weren't a teenager when it took you so long to object to being kissed."

"I was caught on a nail and I thought you were a criminal. Not exactly a situation where one wants to make waves," Sunny said indignantly. "If you're not here to apologize, why are you pestering me again? Don't tell me you don't trust the repairman, either?"

"I came to return this." A piece of hard plastic dropped to the table with a thud.

Sunny stared at the strange, round object. "What is it?"

"The distributor cap to your car."

"You stole the distributor cap from my car? Did it ever occur to you I might want to go somewhere?"

"That was the whole point. I didn't want you to go anywhere." A slight grin touched his lips. "Even if you weren't the world's most inept cat burglar, I only had your word for it that the Reeces wouldn't object to your being here. Plus, your face was white as a ghost. I didn't know how sick you were, so I called Dillon to see if it was OK to leave you here alone."

If Adam Traherne had given Dillon his version of what occurred last night, she could expect an interrogating phone call from Blythe anytime now. Great. She'd ended up next door to the world's busiest-interfering-body. She scowled at him. "Put that thing back in my car and go away. I came to Estes Park to rest, not to be harassed by the likes of you."

"To rest or to be lazy? Dillon said you can't seem to shake the after-effects of your mild," he emphasized the word, "case of flu, even though your doctor says you ought to be completely recovered. You haven't gone back to work, but spend your days laying around. From where I'm standing, it sounds like you're suffering from a good, old-fashioned case of malingering."

The unfair assessment rendered her momentarily speechless. Recovering, she said angrily, "You're standing where you're not wanted. Get out of here right this minute or I'll... And leave that stupid distributor cap right there," she said as he stretched out his hand. "I'll call someone to fix it. I don't trust a man as sick in the head as you are anywhere near my car."

"You're a lot like your sister. She tends to be excitable, too."

"Neither Blythe nor I are the least bit excitable. We do, however, share a strong aversion to smart-aleck, know-it-all idiots. Put that down! You've no right to snoop through my things."

Reaching for the distributor cap, he'd noticed her sketch pad and picked it up. Disregarding her outraged order, he thumbed through the pages, easily fending Sunny off with a stiff arm as she grabbed at the pad. "Black Adam Traherne rubs out the competition for Chicago Lil?" He gave her a look of cool amusement.

Sunny had drawn him blowing smoke from the business end of a machine gun. It wasn't clear if the blond draped across his lap hiding her face in his shoulder was embarrassed at wearing nothing more than a strategically placed bow or was averting her eyes from the sight of the pair of lifeless legs trailing off the edge of the paper. "It was for my own private amusement," Sunny said stiffly.

The next sketch was as outrageous. He was dressed in black from the top of his ten-gallon hat to the bottom of his down-at-the-heel cowboy boots, with a six-gun in one hand and a scantily clad saloon girl in the other. The drawing was in pencil, but no one could doubt the woman's hair flamed fiery red.

"These sketches are very clever." Adam Traherne subjected Sunny to a long appraising look.

She grabbed the pad and shoved it behind her. "I believe you were leaving."

He picked up the distributor cap and absently tossed it from one hand to another. "What is it you do? Cartoonist?"

"I thought you knew. I don't do anything. I'm lazy, a parasite." She forced a saccharine smile to her lips. "You'd better run away before I decide to attach myself to you."

He grinned. "Honey, you're not my type. I like my women blond and leggy with pouty mouths." He paused in the open doorway. "And hypochondriacs bore me." The front door closed behind him.

Sunny slammed the sketch pad down on the table. No wonder Blythe couldn't stand the man. Previously Sunny had assumed Blythe's dislike stemmed from Adam Traherne's rejection of her social invitations, not to mention the incidents categorized by Blythe as "boys being boys," but now Sunny understood precisely from whence Blythe's dislike sprang. Adam Traherne was a totally disagreeable excuse for a human being. Fortunately, now that he'd satisfied himself as to her identity, their paths need never again cross. She hadn't come to Estes to be insulted by a smug, officious, interfering busybody.

A numbing grayness settled over her. Adam Traherne hadn't been that far wrong. What nursing Grumps hadn't taken out of her, the bout of flu had, but the fact remained, there was no physical reason for the fatigue which sapped her will and energy. Convinced she was still too worried about him to properly rest, Grumps had sent her away.

Sunny wondered what Grumps would make of Adam Traherne. The obnoxious busybody was the antithesis of Grumps. Grumps was daylight while Adam Traherne belonged to the night in his black sweatshirt and pants. Grumps was thin and angular, almost bony. The first thing her trained artist's eye had noticed about Adam Traherne was his powerful, muscular figure and the athletic grace of his movements. Grumps was kind and nonthreatening. Adam Traherne was large and intimidating, with an aura of power radiating from his strong body. Calmly self-possessed, he absolutely reeked of masculinity.

OK, she admitted it, he aroused her curiosity. People intrigued her, so naturally she speculated about him. If one ignored his personality, he was an attractive physical specimen. Maybe six feet tall, definitely dark and handsome, and a woman could lose herself in that chin dimple. If a woman liked that sort of thing.

What was the matter with her? The last thing she needed or wanted was a man like him in her life. There was already a surplus of people pushing and pulling at her, giving her advice, trying to run her life. No, she definitely could do without Adam Traherne. Her mistake was in drawing him as some kind of superhero.

Picking up her pad, Sunny began a new series of sketches. A leer, a hangman's knot, an eye patch, a sniveling coward walking the plank... Only the snivel turned into a bold glare of defiance, the leer into cool mockery. Darn, the guy wouldn't even let himself be hung by the neck. Here came a maiden to his rescue. Her legs refused to be long, or her hair blond. Sunny shredded the page and flung the pad across the room, abandoning the straight chair for a more comfortable overstuffed one.

The large pine-framed mirror across the room reflected the image of the woman in the sketch who'd come riding up, six-guns blazing. Where were her brains? Just because the man's chin was bisected by an intriguing dimple...

If there was anyone who lacked the energy or interest to deal with Adam Traherne, it was Sunny Taite. Her life had spun far enough off course as it was. A situation she ought to be figuring out how to rectify. Her sigh echoed loudly in the large, empty room. She closed her eyes; her body crumpled into the chair. Maybe the sun would shine tomorrow.

Heavy footsteps treading across the floor woke her.

"I thought I told you to lock up."

Adam Traherne's accusing voice chased away any lingering dregs of sleep. Sunny mentally counted to ten before attempting civilized conversation. "Would you please quit marching in and out of this house as if it were Grand Central Station?"

"Quit leaving your doors unlocked."

"I don't need a baby-sitter or watchdog or whatever it is you think you are." Her neck was stiff from falling asleep in the chair. "It ought to be obvious even to someone as dense as you that I want to be alone."

He pulled a dining chair from beneath the table and, hauling it toward her, straddled it, his arms resting across the back. "I have a proposition for you."

Sunny attempted to rub soreness from her taut neck muscles. "Oh, please. I've never aspired to long legs or pouty lips, and my hair has never been anything but brown."

His dark eyes filled with cynical amusement. "You certainly jumped without hesitation to that conclusion, but don't get your hopes up. While I might be able to overlook a shrimp-sized frame and mud-colored hair, I'd never prefer a smart-aleck mouth to pouty lips."

The man was impossible. Shutting her eyes, she blocked him out. "Go away."

"I made a few phone calls this afternoon and found out who you really are."

"Sunny Taite." This wasn't a subject she wanted to pursue. Standing up, she walked into the kitchen and poured herself a glass of water.

He dragged the chair back to the table and sat. "One of those sketches I saw this morning triggered a memory, but it proved damned elusive. It wasn't until I was talking to my sister-in-law and she mentioned reading to her daughter that recognition finally came to me. You're Sunny Taite."

"How clever of you to figure it out," she marveled. "Especially since I told you my name is Sunny Taite." She picked up the dishrag and scrubbed an old stain on the countertop.

"The problem was reconciling Sunny Taite the bedraggled intruder with Sunny Taite the author and illustrator of *The Melancholy Apple Prince* and *The Blue Bird In The Banana Tree.*"

"I believe you were leaving." The stain was stubborn.

"You haven't heard my proposition yet."

"But you've heard my answer. No." She carefully rinsed out the rag and draped it neatly over the rim of the sink.

"As I said, I made a few phone calls. I have a friend back east in the publishing business." He stretched his long legs across the floor. "Word on the street is that you have refused to sign any new contracts. He suggested personal problems.''

"I'm not interested in gossip." Water spots on the faucet drew her eye. She polished them off with her sleeve. "What I chose to do or not do is none of your or anyone else's business." Who did he think he was, conducting an inquisition in her sister's kitchen? She moved to the back door and pulled it open. "Goodbye."

He didn't budge. "Five thousand dollars. Shut the door. You're letting the cold air in."

"I beg your pardon." The man was clearly unhinged. Sunny closed the door and leaned against it, her hands grasping the cold knob behind her.

"I'm willing to pay you five thousand dollars for a painting done in the style of your illustrations."

"You mean you want to buy one of the original paintings from one of my books?" Her mind was still befuddled by sleep.

"My sister-in-law loves your picture books for children. She bought extra copies so she could cut out and frame some of the pages for my niece's room. I want you to paint a special picture for my niece, a large portrait of her father."

"I don't do that type of thing. If you want to give your niece something, why don't you buy her a doll or new records or something?"

"She has plenty of dolls and records."

"I'll bet she does. I'll also bet she's a spoiled brat." He couldn't know what he was asking of her, but even so, anger flowed through her body, lending her strength. "Get her a horse or roller blades, then, or does she already have them, too? I suppose it's pretty tough to buy a present for a kid who already has everything."

"She doesn't have a father. He's dead."

The bald statement punched Sunny painfully in the stomach. "Oh." She sank down on the nearest chair. "I'm sorry."

"Why should you be sorry?" He turned his chair so he was facing her. "You weren't the drunk who slammed broadside into my brother's car and killed him."

"I can be sorry it happened. And sympathize with you."

"I'm not asking for your pity. I'm asking you to consider a simple, straightforward, business proposition."

"Whether you want my sympathy or not, my heart goes out to anyone who's lost a loved one." Her hands were tightly folded on the table. "But I'm not interested in painting a picture." She studied the blue lines of her veins. "You'll have to find someone else. The friend you mentioned earlier should be able to help you."

"I don't want to find someone else."

"I'm sorry." She rubbed the base of her thumb. "I know how tragic it is for you to lose a brother and for your niece to lose her father, but—"

"Do you?"

"My father died when I was six. He'd stopped to change a tire and hadn't pulled far enough off the highway." She paused. "I'm sure you mean well, but a painting won't make up for the loss of her father."

His eyes were coldly contemptuous. "I'm not stupid. I don't want a substitute for her father. I want a portrait of him."

"I can't help you."

"All right. I'll pay you ten thousand dollars."

"Money has nothing to do with it. I'm simply not interested."

"Why not? From what Dillon and my friend said, you're not working on anything else."

The calm question and his refusal to drop the matter shattered Sunny's veneer of self-control. Jumping to her feet, she ignored the chair crashing to the floor. "I don't know who you think you are, Mr. Traherne, but you're rude, aggravating and an enormous pain in the neck. I'm sorry about your brother and your niece, but I am not a circus dog to perform at your command. I don't do commissions and I don't do portraits and I don't care if you like pouty blondes, and you can sleep with long-legged flamingos for all I care. Just go away and leave me alone."

Uncoiling his large body from the chair, he rose to his feet. "Sleep on my proposition. You'll see things clearer in the morning." Straightening the chair, he deftly slid it under the table. "You can't spend the rest of your life laying around doing nothing."

"Yes I can."

"Your family has made a mistake in indulging, if not abetting, your malingering." At the door he turned to give her a long, steady look. "I don't believe in catering to weakness. Think about my offer. I'll be back." The door closed behind him.

Moving in slow motion, Sunny set her fallen chair upright and slumped down on it. Adam Traherne was a cold, arrogant, selfish monster. Grumps would tell her to ignore him. She could use some of Grumps's common sense advice about now. Except that she'd promised she wouldn't call him.

Grumps said he knew her, if he talked to her on the phone she'd decide he sounded weak or Esther wasn't feeding him right or some dumb thing. No, he'd declared, Esther was perfectly competent and Sunny was not to worry. He didn't want to see hide nor hair of her or hear the sound of her voice for at least one month.

Tears pooled in her eyes. Dearest Grumps. He'd never admit she'd let him down.

If only she wasn't so tired. If only Adam Traherne would stop bothering her. She wiped the moisture trickling down her cheeks. No matter how hard she wished, Adam Traherne was not going to meekly disappear, but there had to be some way to get rid of him. It was time she found out a little more about him.

The kitchen clock showed seven p.m. Earlier, on the phone, Blythe had said she and a friend were attending a play this evening. Even though it was Saturday, Dillon had been out of town and intended to spend the evening at his office catching up on business matters. Sunny dug the phone number for her brother-in-law's private office line from her wallet.

Sunny's gaze fixed sightlessly on the ceiling, the temporary oblivion of sleep eluding her. It was her own fault for succumbing to a nap this afternoon after promising herself she wouldn't do it again. No, it was his fault, that loutish clod next door. Rubbing her nose in the breakdown of her life. Refusing to leave her in peace. She pulled the blankets up to her chin, but they failed to warm her.

From outside the house came rustling noises and the sound of twigs breaking. Sunny's breath caught before she remembered Dillon telling her that deer and elk came down from the mountains as fall days shortened into winter. Most of the large mammals stayed inside the national park boundaries, but there were always those who preferred the culinary delights to be found in yards along the edges of town.

From the sound, one beast was scratching his rump against the wooden frame of her bedroom window. The image brought a smile to her face. Without arms or fin-

gernails, it couldn't be easy scratching for fleas or ticks.
The animal moved on, and Sunny heard him at the
window in the next bedroom. Scratch, scratch, scratch,
she thought, her eyelids sinking shut.

The next sound Sunny heard was a thunderous din at
her back door. Fumbling for her glasses, she stuck them
on her nose and squinted at the clock. It was almost
midnight. The banging at the back door increased, and
a voice shouted her name. Throwing back the covers,
she jumped out of bed and hurried down the hall in her
bare feet. At the door she halted. "Who is it?"

"Adam Traherne. You OK in there?"

"Of course. Why wouldn't I be?"

"I've caught a prowler. Let me in."

Turning on the kitchen light, Sunny cautiously opened
the door.

Adam Traherne held a struggling figure firmly in his
grasp. "There's more foot traffic around this house than
on Denver's 16th Street Mall. It was lucky I happened
to look out the window. This hoodlum was skulking
around your house. Knowing your cavalier attitude
toward door locks..." He thrust his captive into the
room. "I caught him as he was getting ready to smash
a window with a rock."

"Why don't you mind your own business?" the intruder asked sullenly. "It's my house."

For the first time, Sunny looked at the accused
prowler. "Bud! What are you doing here?"

Adam Traherne gave the youth a sharp look. "Well,
hell," he said in disgust. "One of the Reece kids. I should
have known. Breaking and entering seems to be one of
your family's chief pastimes." He pushed Bud onto a
nearby chair. "Your nephew is stinking drunk."

"Don't be ridiculous. Bud's only sixteen."

Bud gave her an owlish stare. "What are you doing here, Sunny? Nobody told me you were here. I thought you were coming to Denver."

Sunny's eyes narrowed and she stepped closer to her nephew and sniffed. "Never mind what I'm doing here. What are you doing here? You smell like a brewery."

"Only had a couple of beers," Bud said in a slurred voice.

Adam Traherne sat down at the table, his arms across his chest. "He'll probably be sick."

Sunny gave him a dirty look before turning back to Bud. "Does your mother know you're up here?"

Bud gave her a cunning grin. "She thinks I'm spending the night at Matt's." He slid further down on his chair. "Jenny's supposed to be spending the night at Allison's."

"Jenny?" Sunny asked.

"Bud. I don't feel so well." A woebegone voice spoke from the open doorway.

"Jenny," Adam Traherne said in a resigned voice.

Bud frowned at the newcomer. "I told you not to have that last beer," he said, carefully enunciating each word.

"I..." The girl covered her mouth with both hands.

Sunny rushed her down the hall to the bathroom. By the time Sunny had held Jenny's hand, cleaned her up, comforted her and tucked her into a spare bed, she was furious with her nephew. Throwing on her bathrobe, Sunny stalked into the kitchen, drawing and quartering on her mind. Adam Traherne was sitting alone at the table, a mug of coffee in front of him. His presuming to make himself at home in her kitchen gave her the perfect outlet for an anger born of fright. "Why are you still here?"

"Waiting to see if you need help."

"I don't need any help from you. Where's Bud?"

"His girlfriend's race down the hall preceded his by only a matter of seconds. Since you had your hands full, I made up one of the beds in the other bedroom and threw him in it after he'd finished tossing his cookies."

"I suppose I'm expected to thank you for that?"

He shrugged. "Suit yourself."

"And you needn't expect any thanks for capturing a big, bad burglar, either," she added ungraciously. "Even I could have handled a drunk teenager." Drunk. The staggering implications hit her again, and she turned away to grip the edge of the countertop, striving for control.

"Take it easy." Heavy hands grasped her shoulders and moved her aside. "I'll fix you some instant coffee."

Nightmarish visions paraded obscenely through her head. "They could have been killed," she whispered. "When I think of that road, the sharp curves, the deep canyon..." Attempting to control her trembling, she cradled in her hands the hot mug he thrust at her.

"Except for a Grade-A headache in the morning, he'll be OK."

"How could Bud be so stupid? I'm so angry I could, I could..." She bit down hard on her lower lip.

"I know." Wresting the mug from her frozen fingers, he set it on the counter and wrapped strong arms around her.

Sunny knew she ought to break away, but having someone warm and solid to lean on, even an irritating stranger, was such a comfort that she momentarily surrendered to the need. Eyes closed, she felt the warmth from his chest and arms seep into her bones, dispelling the shivers which threatened each time she thought of what might have happened.

Gradually the steady beat of his heart and the slow, even tempo of his breathing calmed her. With the nightmare under control came the embarrassing realization that she was locked in the embrace of a man she hardly knew and didn't like. She stepped back from him with an embarrassed laugh. "I suppose now you're convinced I'm a complete idiot."

He handed Sunny her coffee. "At least you had your door locked."

"Would you stop with your stupid fixation on that stupid door's stupid lock!"

He pressed her down on the nearest chair and sat across the table from her. "Keeping your doors locked is a matter of common sense. A commodity which your family appears to possess in only minute amounts, if at all."

The man was the most self-righteous, maddening person she'd ever come across. The fact that his erroneous conclusion was based on incontrovertible evidence failed to excuse him. "You've done your good deed for the day. Why don't you go home?"

"What are you going to do about the kid?"

"That's none of your business, is it?"

"You know, of course, why he got that poor girl drunk and brought her up here. Raging hormones."

"You don't have to make it sound as if he kidnapped her," Sunny objected. "Bud's only sixteen."

"He's old enough to drive a car, obtain liquor illegally, and plan a seduction."

"The girl is sixteen, too."

"I'm sure she was a willing participant, but that doesn't lessen either's culpability. The alcohol was undoubtedly intended to give them both courage. They acted like idiots and behaved with an immature disregard for the consequences."

"Save your fancy lawyer speeches for court. I'll—"

"Lawyer speeches?"

"You checked on me. I checked on you. No matter what your opinion of me, I do not lack common sense. The fact that you acted rude and surly and had a key to this house didn't prove you were Dillon's neighbor." Sunny gripped her mug. "Although I should have figured out you weren't a burglar the minute you kissed me."

"You do go on about that kiss," he said mildly.

"I'm not going on about anything. I'm merely pointing out a burglar would be more interested in a speedy exit than slobbering over bystanders."

"Slobbering," he repeated. "Do I detect a hint of criticism about my technique? Perhaps I wasn't..." He paused. "Inspired."

"I'm aware you need long-legged blondes for inspiration. Since there aren't any around here, you may as well go home."

"What do you intend to do about your nephew?"

Her stomach lurched. How could she have forgotten Bud for even a second? Her brain was totally dead. Convincing an adolescent male of the error of his ways would take more energy and tact than she felt capable of, but she wasn't about to admit it. "I'll talk to him, and explain—"

"That Auntie Sunny doesn't approve of his behavior." Adam Traherne finished her statement in a derisive voice. "He was so inebriated, he's lucky they made it up here. Do the kid a favor and treat this as serious as it is. He's old enough to be responsible for his actions."

"I know that," Sunny said defensively. "I just need to think what to do. It's after one a.m. Blythe and Dillon think Bud's spending the night at a friend's, and they're probably sound asleep." Thinking out loud, she traced the rim of the mug with her finger. "The only thing calling them would accomplish is ruining their sleep. The kids are safely tucked into bed.''

''This time.'' His steady gaze weighed her across the wide expanse of wooden table. ''What about the next time?''

Sunny chewed her lip indecisively. ''Bud would hate me for telling tales on him.''

''Then don't say anything. Dead men can't hate.''

The harsh statement drove the blood from her head. Shakily she said, ''That's a very cruel thing to say.''

''Letting him get away with irresponsible behavior because you want to stay on his good side is a cruel way to behave. Not to mention spineless and selfish. So much for your unstinting family devotion and self-sacrifice that Dillon raved about.'' He leaned back in his chair. ''You must not care much for your nephew. Not when you're more concerned about being liked than whether he lives or dies.''

Sunny swayed from the impact of his words. ''That is the meanest, most despicable...'' Her voice was low and fierce. ''I'd never deliberately behave in any way that might jeopardize Bud's well-being.''

''Then give the kid a break.'' He drained his mug. ''And don't treat this as some kind of teenage prank.''

''Despite what you obviously believe, Mr. Traherne, I am not some addle-brained twit too dumb to know the difference between silly horseplay and dangerously stupid behavior. And I do not appreciate your intimating that I am.'' She shoved back her chair and stood up. ''Once and for all, go away and leave me alone!''

He rose to his feet, annoyance furrowing his brow. ''You think I enjoy running over here to rescue you every five minutes? I have better things to do than play nanny to an irresponsible, rash, self-centered, pint-sized nitwit.''

"And I have better things to do than listen to the ignorant ranting and raving of a pompous, meddling do-gooder. I am perfectly capable of dealing with this situation, and any others that arise—" she jammed her fists on her hips and glared across the table "—without any help or interference from you."

"Good." He strolled around the large table to where she stood. "Remember that the next time you find yourself nailed to a window or needing a shoulder to cry on."

"I wasn't crying." Refusing to be intimidated by the huge hulk looming over her, Sunny drew herself up to her full five feet three inches. "And if I was, your shoulder would be the last I'd want. I prefer my men to be halfway human, not self-righteous, judgmental automatons who wouldn't recognize an emotion if it kicked them in the knees."

"A friend of mine once had a Chihuahua. Pepper was a feisty little dog small enough to fit in a shoebox, but willing to take on the whole world." He took possession of one of Sunny's braids and slowly brushed the end up the side of her neck and face. "I could never decide if she was brave or ridiculous, but she was cute in an oddball sort of way."

Sunny wouldn't have believed a person's eyes could change so rapidly from cold contempt to warm amusement, and the transformation fascinated her. That could be the only explanation for what happened next. Or maybe it was the oddly attractive wry grin curving Adam Traherne's lips that held her motionless as he lifted the glasses from her face and laid them on the table.

"I thought you were leaving," she said breathlessly. Not even the most insecure man in the world would take that as a protest against being kissed. Adam Traherne was definitely not insecure.

CHAPTER THREE

HE TASTED of coffee. A mind-drugging coffee that eroded Sunny's will and sapped her strength. A steel arm held her securely against a warm, solid chest that thudded with a steady beat. His breathing echoed in her ears; his breath fluttered against her face. With one hand he caressed her scalp with the barest of pressure. Sunny clutched at his shoulders and shivered. With the plundering of her mouth, unfamiliar sensations cascaded down her spine.

He abandoned her lips to nibble his way along her chin line, his mouth burning her skin. His fingers slipped beneath the neckline of her nightshirt, tugging it to one side. Kisses rained up the side of her neck, returning to the corner of her lips. Then he lifted his head, and she felt him looking down at her. She concentrated on the center of his chest. He was wearing a black cable-knit sweater.

"I suppose you kissed me to prove some sort of macho point," she said.

"I wish I had," he said ruefully, flipping one of her brown braids over her shoulder. "But as much as I hate to admit it, the truth is, you looked so damned cute and funny standing there spitting fire at me, I couldn't help myself."

The amused explanation deepened her humiliation. "I'm happy my size and behavior entertain you."

"Would you be less annoyed if I admitted the joke's on me?" He brushed a straying strand of hair away from her cheek. "I thought I'd outgrown being distracted by a damned mountain sprite with honey-dipped lips."

His hand still rested lightly against her cheek, and Sunny closed her eyes, fighting off an irrational urge to melt into his skin. Allowing him to kiss her had been insane. She had to say something.

"I apologize if my actions have given you a mistaken impression, Mr. Traherne. This has been an upsetting evening. I don't normally..." She forced herself to meet his gaze. "Do stuff like that."

"Adam." His eyes gleamed down at her. "After the way you kissed me, I think you'd better call me Adam."

"You kissed me, Mr. Traherne."

"A kiss like that requires two. Call me Adam."

"I admit I, uh, did participate somewhat in the exercise." She ignored his snort. "But I don't intend to repeat the error, and since we will never see each other again, I see no reason to call you anything at all." She picked up her glasses and resettled them firmly on her face.

"Armor?" He tapped the nosepiece of her glasses. "Or a case of the better to see the big bad wolf?"

"If you're implying I'm frightened of you, you're wrong." The look he gave her made it clear he didn't believe her. "Good-night, Mr. Traherne."

"Adam." He reached for the doorknob. "I'll see you in the morning. There's still the little matter of my business proposition to be discussed."

The door closed behind him before Sunny could find her voice. Of all the outrageous, blatantly manipulative, egomaniacs... What a smirking grin he'd worn when he told her to call him Adam. The only names she wanted to call him were ones her mother would be horrified to learn Sunny knew.

Adam Traherne hadn't kissed her because he found her cute or appealing or anything else. Marching over to the back door, she slammed the lock in place. He'd kissed her because he thought she was so stupid and naive a gorilla could influence her with one stupid, sloppy kiss. Influence her to paint his stupid picture. He wasn't interested in anything else about her. He hadn't the faintest desire to crawl into her bed. Not that she wanted him there. Which he probably thought she did.

How mortifying she'd returned his kiss. He hadn't tied her down or held a gun to her head. The worst of it was, she'd actually enjoyed it. Pacing the length of the kitchen floor, Sunny wondered if her recent flu could have affected her brain.

Adam Traherne might be physically attractive in a dark, satanic sort of way, but he wasn't her type. He'd merely caught her in a weak moment. She'd surrendered to a brief, harmless, totally understandable urge to be held and comforted at a time of intense anxiety. That's all it was. Only in fairy tales did kissing a toad turn him into a prince.

She went back to bed, but the problem of her houseguests loomed large. It went against the grain to agree with a toad, but Adam Traherne was right to stress the need for Bud to understand the severity of his transgressions. All she had to do was figure out how to bring about the desired state of understanding. Easy, until one remembered lately she'd barely been capable of deciding whether getting out of bed in the morning was worth the effort.

Sunny rolled over on her stomach, smothering an insidious weakness that whispered Adam Traherne might have helped. According to Dillon, Adam Traherne was an up-and-coming defense attorney who was building a national reputation. He probably possessed some insight into a criminal mind. Not that Bud was a criminal. He was merely a silly teenager. So what if Adam Traherne undoubtedly had scads of experience with juvenile delinquents? Adam Traherne undoubtedly had scads of experience with a number of things, women heading a long list.

Sitting up in bed, Sunny tucked her knees under her chin. Moonlight flooded the room, enabling her dimly to see herself in the mirror on the opposite wall. No makeup, loose strands of hair flying every which way and a worn nightshirt proclaiming her college allegiance. She was a mess. One look at her and Adam Traherne had undoubtedly believed it would be a cinch to manipulate her with a kiss or two. She grimaced at her twin in the mirror. It was past time he learned not all women could be manipulated with a kiss, no matter how masterful or mind-numbing.

Sunny punched her pillow into shape, wishing the soft mass was Adam Traherne's mouth. Not that there was anything soft about his mouth. On the contrary, it was as firm and solid as the rest of him. She flopped down on her back and yanked the covers into place. The solidest part of Adam Traherne was his granite brain. And hers must be pure mush. Darn that man. Her problem was what to do about Bud, not what to do about Adam Traherne. She didn't intend to do anything about him except ignore him.

Shutting her eyes, Sunny sketched in an imaginary sketchbook. Adam Traherne tied to a stake, tall, long-legged blondes with pouty mouths dancing wildly around him as he watched with approval.

The prancing blondes metamorphosed into leaping flames, and in their midst appeared a sexy-looking, brown-haired goddess, her slight frame dressed in flowing black, her small stature augmented by stiletto heels. Ignoring the conflagration, Adam Traherne gave the witch a slow, deeply sensual smile. His dark eyes mocked her limited powers as she flung assorted curses upon him. Plague, pestilence and poisonous lizards. Sunny fell asleep to the sound of her own malevolent laughter ringing in her ears.

Ringing. Sunny opened her eyes. Early morning light crept across the ceiling. A sense of disquiet tugged at the edges of her fogged brain, and then memories of the previous evening flooded back. Bud. No wonder she failed to feel rested. A sharp ring tore through the house. The door bell. Reaching out blindly, Sunny found her glasses and peered at the clock. Seven in the morning. She stumbled out of bed. A quick check showed Bud and Jenny still dead to the world. The door bell rang again and continued to ring. Whoever was at the door at this ungodly hour must have a thumb glued to the bell.

Sunny threw open the front door.

"It's about time."

"Time! Do you know what time it is?"

"Yes. Do you?" Adam Traherne strode past her into the house. "That's what you were wearing the last time I saw you."

"I sleep in this." Yawning widely, she trailed him into the kitchen. "It's called a nightshirt. Sleeping is what I do at night."

"I wouldn't brag about it." He set a bulging brown paper bag on the countertop. "Have you had breakfast?"

Her mind was still sluggish. "What in the world are you doing?" The sight of Bud's car keys on the table acted as a wake-up call. How dare this man march in here as if he were welcome! "My eating habits are none of your business."

"You were lolling around in bed," he said accusingly, opening her refrigerator. "I see you went to the grocery store. Whole milk, eggs, bacon. No wonder you behave like a nitwit. Your brain must be clogged with cholesterol and fat."

Sunny gave him a look of pure dislike. "Thank you, Dr. Traherne, for the latest health update. Take all that junk—" she indicated the food he was removing from the sack "—and go home. I'm having coffee and a doughnut for breakfast."

"The name is Adam." He found a skillet and banged it down on a burner. "You're having orange juice, apple yogurt pancakes, turkey sausage, and fresh fruit."

"Turkey sausage sounds disgusting, and I don't remember inviting you—"

"How many pancakes?"

"None. Would you please get out of—"

"You have fifteen minutes to get dressed." He stopped rummaging in the paper sack and frowned at her. "What are you waiting for?" When she stared speechlessly at him, he ordered, "Move, before I remember beneath your nightshirt is nothing but you."

Sunny moved. It was difficult, if not impossible, to maintain one's dignity while standing barefoot, open-mouthed, and dressed in an oversize, ancient nightshirt. She was going to need every shred of dignity she'd ever hoped to possess to convince this imbecile from next door he was never to darken her doorstep again. Furthermore, no turkey sausage was going to pass her lips, she vowed, stepping into the shower. It sounded as revolting as Adam Traherne.

Scrubbing her wet hair with a towel after a quick shower, Sunny decided getting rid of the man in her kitchen came first; then she'd deal with the problem of Bud. She swiftly plaited her damp hair in a single braid, which she twisted up and skewered to the back of her head. A spicy odor drifted down the hallway. Adam Traherne was leaving and taking his turkey sausage with him.

Breakfast was eaten in silence. Getting rid of blood-sucking leeches would be easier than getting rid of this man. And his sausage. Not that the sausage was so awful.

"Tastes pretty good, doesn't it?"

"It was edible." She shoved her plate aside. "Go home. I'll do the dishes." Checking his reaction to her rudeness, she peeked across the table through lowered lashes.

He was studying her. "Contact lenses?"

"No wonder you have a reputation for brilliance."

"You look older with your hair up like that."

"You didn't pound on my door at dawn to discuss my hairstyle or to cook me breakfast. And it's difficult to believe you would go to such lengths simply to irritate me. Why are you here?"

Holding his mug between his hands, he leaned his elbows on the table. "You know why I'm here. The portrait."

"And you know what my answer is. No."

"Tell me about the old man you were caring for."

"No." Sunny stood up and gathered the dirty dishes to carry them to the sink.

"Why not?" Adam Traherne handed her the en-crusted skillet.

"I don't want to talk to you anymore. Because I want you to go away. Because a man like you could never understand how it is with Grumps and me." She glared at him. "You've probably never cared about anyone but yourself, so that kind of closeness is undoubtedly some-thing you know nothing about."

"Don't I?"

The haunted look which briefly shadowed his eyes reminded her this man had lost his only brother in a tragic accident. Adam Traherne might behave like a boor, but she didn't have to emulate him. Embarrassed and appalled by her nasty words, Sunny attacked the dirty skillet with a vengeance. He had cooked her breakfast.

"I was twelve when Mother married Martin. All four of my grandparents were dead before I was born, so I could hardly wait to meet Nolan, Martin's father. I pictured him as a cross between Santa Claus and a fairy godmother." Her soapy hands stilled. "When Nolan came for the wedding I heard him tell Martin that Martin was a fool to marry a woman with a preteen. Nolan went on and on about the problems of raising a teenager. And I grew madder and madder until I burst into Martin's study and told Nolan he was the most horrible person in the world."

Martin's father was a tall, thin, balding man with wire-framed glasses and brown eyes that seemed to pierce right through her. Nothing like the blue-eyed, roly-poly Grandpa she'd imagined.

"In my best twelve-year-old manner, I loftily informed him I'd been going to call him Gramps but since he was so horrid, I was going to call him Grumps."

"What did he say?" Taking the dripping skillet from her idle hands, he rinsed and dried it.

"He asked if I played chess. When I said I didn't, he told me it was time I learned. I was sixteen before I won a game." A tear escaped down her cheek, and she wiped at it, leaving a streak of cool suds. "This year... He almost died." The last words were little more than a whisper.

"But he didn't." Adam wiped the soapsuds from her face. "What was wrong with him? Dillon didn't say."

"He was on his daily walk. As he was about to cross the street, a squirrel being chased by a cat came from nowhere, startling Grumps and he fell. He tore up his knee and had to have arthroscopic surgery."

"Knee surgery hardly sounds life-threatening."

"A couple of days after he got home, I found him coughing up blood, and rushed him to the hospital. He'd had a pulmonary embolus. A blood clot in his leg had broken loose and gone to his lungs. They put him immediately on an IV." Dirty dishwater drained noisily from the sink. "If I hadn't found him . . . a second pulmonary embolus could have killed him."

"But you did find him."

"He should never have had the clot in his calf. It was caused by the blood pooling. I should have been massaging his calf and leg. I knew his knee hurt when he moved, but I should have made him get out of bed and exercise. Instead I gave him drinks, food, the phone, the TV remote control—everything he could possibly want or need. I told him to call me if he needed me, and then I went upstairs to my studio and went to work."

He frowned. "I'm surprised the hospital didn't make it clear to him how important it was he get up and move around."

"Of course they told him," Sunny said impatiently, "but his knee hurt. I was taking care of him. It was up to me to find out what Grumps's doctor's orders were and make sure Grumps followed them."

"I don't think you need to beat yourself over the head. The man is an adult. He made his own choices."

After a moment, Sunny said carefully, "Yes, of course. You're right. And now he's out of danger, it really doesn't matter anyway."

"That's right." Adam moved away, three long strides taking him to the windowed wall. Looking toward the mountains, he said, "The important thing is, he's alive."

Unlike Adam's brother. The unspoken words seemed to hang in the air. The towel in her hands forgotten, Sunny stared at Adam Traherne's rigid back. "One minute Grumps was asking me if I wanted to go for a walk, and the next a neighbor called to tell me Grumps had gone to the hospital in an ambulance. The unexpectedness of it..." Slowly she added, "A sudden, traumatic death must be shattering."

"Yes." He turned toward her, his empty gaze fixed on a beam over her head. "One minute you have a brother, the next minute you don't. The end to shared plans, to so many things. Never again to bet with him on a football game, to argue politics with him, to hear him laugh... You think of things you wish you'd told him. You wonder if he knew how important he was..." The deliberately emotionless voice betrayed a profound grief.

Sunny felt if she were trespassing. A long moment passed before she trusted her voice. "Dillon said your brother was two years younger than you." Adam Traherne transferred the vacant stare to her face. Sunny had the feeling, until her words, he'd totally forgotten her presence.

Visibly he sloughed off the tension riding his shoulders. A slow, predatory smile disclosed strong, white teeth. "If I'd known last night how interested you are in my life story, I'd have stayed and fascinated you with the details." His eyes gleamed. "Although, judging from the way you kissed me, I doubt we'd have spent much time talking."

The fence was back in place, Keep Out signs posted. Turning her back to him, Sunny hung up the dish towel.

"That silly little kiss must have meant a lot more to you than it did to me. I barely remember it."

"I'll be happy..." he placed his hands on the countertop, a solid arm on either side of her, penning her in "...to refresh your memory."

She held herself very still, not willing to risk brushing against him. "That's not necessary." His after-shave, musky with a hint of spice, teased her senses.

"Because you haven't forgotten?" He slid his hands up her arms to her shoulders.

Through her sweater, his hands warmed her skin. His breath stirred the hair on her neck. "Because I have more important things to do than play games with you."

"Afraid?" Turning her toward him, he used his body to press her against the sink.

"No." The cold, hard steel dug into the small of her back.

"The ability to recognize when a person is lying is a great asset to a successful trial lawyer. And—" cool arrogance threaded his voice "—I'm very successful."

She warded him off, her palms flat against his chest. He was wearing another black sweatshirt. Faded, well-worn, the fabric was soft and warm beneath her hands. His body would be as warm and smooth, but not soft. Through her artist's fingertips she felt the elastic toughness of sinew. His body was a work of art. Not the lean, elongated lines of El Greco's subjects, but the muscular beauty and strength of Michelangelo's *David*.

He was watching her, waiting for her answer. What were they discussing? Oh, yes, lying. She wished she could lift an eyebrow in mockery the way he did. "Does bragging about your professional prowess usually impress women?"

The shaft missed its mark. One corner of his mouth slanted upward. "Makes 'em putty in my hands."

"It won't work on me."

"No?" He clamped his hands over hers, holding them securely against his chest. "What does work on you?"

Sunny tipped her head to one side, as if considering her answer. Adam Traherne needed his self-assurance dented. "Tall lean men with wavy blond hair. And baby blue eyes. I positively melt at the sight of baby blue eyes." She fluttered her eyelashes, before adding crisply, "Since you're not my type, why don't you unhand me and toddle off home like a good boy?"

"Unhand you? How melodramatic." He laughed softly. "You don't have a lick of good sense, do you? Didn't your big sister ever warn you about challenging someone twice your size?"

Too late, Sunny realized that eyes bright with laughter were dangerously seductive. Blood pulsed at the base of her throat and beneath her ears. Bandying words with this man was like drinking a heady elixir of danger and exhilaration. He was right; she was challenging him to kiss her again. Was she out of her mind? She shook her head to clear it. That darned dimple in his chin softened her brain and her knees. Taking an enormous breath, she attempted to free her hands. "Let go of me."

"Say please."

"Let her go and pick on someone your own size."

Sunny would have laughed if Bud hadn't been deadly serious.

Adam Traherne released her and moved across the room. Pouring some coffee, he held it out to Bud. "How's the head?"

Bud slapped aside the proffered mug, ignoring the coffee splashing to the floor. "C'mon, mister. You think you're so tough, picking on a defenseless woman." He gave a credible imitation of a sneer. "Let's see how brave you are with a man."

Indecision paralyzed Sunny. Bud might be six feet tall, but he was only sixteen years old, and she doubted he weighed one hundred and twenty pounds sopping wet. Adam Traherne must outweigh him by at least sixty pounds. He'd pulverize Bud, but throwing her body between them would be as disastrous to Bud's self-esteem. She turned to the large man, a plea hovering on her lips. "Mr. Traherne..."

He looked at her, his face expressionless, his eyes hooded. "If the kid thinks he's old enough to drink, he's too old to hide behind his aunt's skirts."

"I'm not a kid, and I'm not hiding behind Sunny."

With deliberate care Adam Traherne set the mug on the counter and wiped his hands on the kitchen towel. "Sit down before you fall down." With his foot, he hooked a chair out from under the table.

"While I admire your instant defense of your aunt, you can take off your boxing gloves." He refilled the coffee mug and set it in front of Bud and then topped off his own mug. "She can hold her own, even if she is only half grown and thinks I'm a combination of Dillinger and Jesse James, and that—" his lips thinned "—I notch my gun by beating up kids."

He'd been insulted she judged him the kind of man who'd hit a smaller, younger person, Sunny realized. She attempted an apology. "I didn't mean, that is, well, you have..." He'd what? Carried out his neighborly obligation to watch Dillon's house? Just because he rubbed against her like sandpaper against the grain didn't make him a physical bully. "You have to admit you're irritating," she finally said.

He answered coolly. "So are you."

Bud squinted across the table. "Don't I know you? Yeah. You're the jerk from next door."

"I'm also the jerk who held your head last night while you were exceedingly ill." Without looking at Sunny, he added, "Better give him a couple of aspirin."

"If you're planning on giving me a big sermon, save your breath." Bud swallowed the tablets. "There's no way you can improve on what Mom's gonna say. I'm surprised she didn't drive up last night," he added sullenly.

"Why would she?" Adam asked.

"Moms get their kicks from harping on stuff."

"Bud Reece! Your mother loves you," Sunny said indignantly.

"I suppose if your mom was playing Russian roulette," Adam circled the top of his mug with his fingers, "you'd sit on the sidelines and cheer her on."

Bud gave Adam a hostile look. "It's not the same thing. Anyway, it's none of your business."

"You're right. It's none of my business. Want more coffee?"

"It isn't like I did anything wrong," Bud said, goaded by Adam's neutral response into defending himself.

"I didn't say you did. I merely suggested drinking and driving is a form of Russian roulette. Dangerous, yes. But wrong?" He eyed Bud steadily across the table.

"Of course it's wrong," Sunny said.

Adam sent a repressive stare in Sunny's direction. "That's for Bud to decide, isn't it?"

"Sure. Tell my mother that." Bud turned to Sunny. "What did she say when you called her?"

"I haven't called her," Sunny said.

Bud looked at her hopefully. "Does that mean you aren't going to tell her?"

"I haven't decided." Sunny avoided looking at Adam.

"You've put Sunny in quite a spot. Suppose she doesn't tell your parents and next month or next year, you do the same thing and something tragic happens. Your folks would never forgive her." Adam Traherne gave the teenager a challenging look. "I thought you weren't hiding behind her skirts."

"What's it to you what I did?" Bud asked, the sulky note back in his voice. "So I had a couple of drinks...what's the big deal?"

"The big deal is that drunk drivers kill."

"I didn't kill anybody. Why are you making such a federal case out of it? It's nothing to you."

"Bud," Sunny said in a warning voice.

"My brother was killed by a drunk driver," Adam Traherne said evenly.

Bud collapsed like a flat tire. "Jeez, I'm sorry. That's tough. No wonder you're so mad at me."

"I don't care about you one way or the other. If you want to kill yourself, go ahead. Just don't take your friends and innocent bystanders with you."

"Mr. Traherne!" Sunny was appalled. "He's just a kid."

"I'm not a kid."

"Good. Then Sunny won't have to tell your folks."

"You can't decide that. He's my nephew."

Looking gratefully at Adam, Bud ignored Sunny's heated protest. "Jeez, thanks. I promise—"

Adam held up his hand. "Sunny won't have to tell them, because you'll tell them yourself."

"You're crazy. They'll murder me." Bud met Adam's level gaze across the table for a long minute and then a sickly grin wobbled across his lips. "I get it. Be a man, rites of passage and junk like that, huh?"

"To manhood." Adam toasted him with his coffee mug.

Bud gave him a calculated look. "You gonna check to see if I tell 'em?"

Adam lifted a inquisitive brow. "Isn't your word good enough?"

"Yeah. Jeez, thanks, Mr. Traherne. I won't let you down."

The man across the table nodded. "Good. And, Bud..." He hesitated, slanting a look at Sunny. "Sleeping with women is a pretty serious step no matter how old a man is. A person needs to consider it very carefully. When you are positive you're ready to take that step, you better hit the drugstore first. Real men use protection."

"Mr. Traherne!" Sunny gasped.

Bud's face erupted in red. "I'll do that, Mr. Traherne." His face turning even grander hues of crimson, his voice cracking, he added, "Let me give you some advice. You may think my brothers and me are a nuisance now, but, well, just don't mess with Sunny. If she doesn't want to kiss you, she doesn't have to. She's had a hard enough time with Grumps in the hospital and then being sick herself and all."

"Bud!" Sunny didn't know whether to laugh or scream.

Adam did neither. He looked straight at Bud and said firmly, "I have no intention of hurting your aunt. I merely want a portrait painted by Sunny Taite."

Which certainly put into perspective those unwanted kisses he'd crammed down Sunny's throat.

CHAPTER FOUR

SUNNY settled comfortably into the lumpy cushions and set the phone on the floor beside the faded chintz chair, her concern about Bud dispelled by her brother-in-law's phone call. Dillon had expressed a comical mixture of outrage at his son's behavior, pride at his confession, and regret that Sunny had been disturbed.

Missing from the conversation was any mention of Adam Traherne. Doubtlessly Bud had preferred to give the impression that his confession had been prompted by his own conscience. Pleased and relieved that Bud had followed through on his promise, Sunny didn't care how he'd packaged his confession. Adam Traherne's name hadn't been mentioned by her, either.

Blythe was distressed enough without learning a man she already disliked on account of her boys was now privy to the knowledge that her eldest son had acted like an idiot. Blythe didn't take kindly to humiliation. Nor would she take kindly to hearing Adam Traherne apparently ran tame in her mountain lodge. Especially when her baby sister was staying there. Not that Blythe needed to worry.

The house was quiet. Sunny propped her feet on a worn leather stool. The window to her right framed a modern, two-story, cedar house. Tall with graying towers, jutting decks and window walls angled to catch the best views, the house reminded her of the old mines that dotted the Colorado mountains. Stark, linear remnants of a historical past, the mines served as testimonials to the strong, rugged miners who'd built them.

Hard, determined men. Men from the same mold as the tenant of the cedar house. Adam Traherne.

The man who'd butted into her family affairs this morning. Granted, the way he'd dealt with Bud had produced the desired outcome, and she had neither the objectivity nor the experience to deal with a teenage nephew under such circumstances.

Still, Adam might have consulted with her before taking charge. How could he have been so certain Bud would keep his word and tell his parents? Dillon claimed much of Adam Traherne's success in getting his clients declared innocent was based on Adam's ability to spot a liar and his refusal to take on a client who lied to him. Maybe hours of courtroom experience had taught Adam a sense of who could be trusted to keep his word.

Sunny shifted to accommodate worn springs. She wouldn't care to be on the witness stand being grilled by Adam Traherne. She had a feeling he didn't quit until he achieved his goal. Which made his leaving after his conversation with Bud surprising. Unless he'd finally realized Sunny could be every bit as stubborn as he. It was a relief to know he'd finally accepted her refusal to paint the portrait. She closed her eyes. Too little sleep had come her way last night.

"You leave your doors unlocked just to irritate me, don't you?" Adam Traherne loomed over the back of her chair, his arms folded across a wide expanse of chest, a censorious look on his face as she blinked up at him.

"My tactic appears to be successful."

He frowned. "Crime is not confined to the inner city."

"Neither, apparently, are you. What do you want now?" Before he could answer, her conscience nudged her into making a begrudging acknowledgment of his good deed. "Dillon called. Bud confessed and threw himself on his parents' mercy. I couldn't have handled him as competently as you, so thanks."

"Gratitude so graciously bestowed can be answered only with an equally warm and sincere, 'You're welcome.'"

Sunny felt her face flame at his mocking voice. Why did this man have the ability to turn her into a surly teenager? Gripping her hands in her lap, she tried again. "I would have ranted and raved at him, and he would have totally ignored me, so I appreciate your help and expertise."

"Even though it galls you to admit it."

She gave him a dirty look. "Even though."

"Your problem is you've been cooped up here since you arrived Friday night. You need some fresh air."

"My problem is getting rid of you."

"Then you've got one hell of a problem. The only way you're going to get rid of me is agree to paint the portrait. Let's go for a drive and talk about it."

She ignored the hand held out to assist her from the deep chair. "There's nothing to talk about. I've made up my mind."

"Being the kind of person who makes up her mind before hearing all the facts is nothing to brag about."

"I'm not bragging, and besides, what other facts are there?"

He studied her, a brooding look on his face. "Have you ever been to Bear Lake?"

"I don't even know what a Bear Lake is. I've only been to Estes Park once before, shortly after Blythe and Dillon bought this place two summers ago. Grumps and I had planned to come this last summer, but—we didn't." She stared across the room at the fireplace, embarrassed by the wobble in her voice.

"Then you have a treat in store for you. Let's go."

"Thank you for asking, but I prefer to stay here."

"I wasn't asking." He pulled her to her feet. "Get a jacket."

"Why should I?" she asked childishly.

"Because the wind blowing off the lake can be frigid."

"That isn't what I meant and you know it."

"All right. You should go to keep me company."

"I'm not in the mood to be good company."

"Then you should indulge me for professional reasons. I'm putting business your way."

"I'm not the least interested in your business, so there's no reason for me to go."

"An ill-mannered clod might mention I did you a favor this morning, but since I pride myself on my sophisticated manners—" he gave her a twisted grin "—I won't suggest you're under any obligation to return the favor." Ignoring her sputtering, he added, "Instead I'll point out I'm larger than you and hauling you out to my car wouldn't be beyond my abilities."

"Or against your personal code of ethics, either, because you obviously don't have one." Sunny stomped to the back door and yanked her jacket from the hook.

He ushered her out the door, murmuring, "I was rather looking forward to slinging you over my shoulder."

Sunny sat stiffly in the front seat, seething as Adam drove his expensive sportscar down Bull Elk Road and turned onto the highway. Although the mountains around them were snow-covered, the autumn afternoon was sunny and mild. A pair of magpies glided past as they stopped at the entrance to Rocky Mountain National Park.

Adam broke off his whistling to pay the park fee. "When my spirits are sagging, nothing can lift me out of the doldrums like coming to this place."

"I don't need any sagging spirits lifted."

"You don't want to lift your spirits," he corrected her. "You obviously enjoy wallowing in your depressing self-absorption."

"Thank you, Sigmund Freud, for your in-depth psychoanalysis. Not that I recall asking you for it. Why don't you leave me in peace and go badger some poor soul who might be misguided enough to welcome your meddling?"

They were driving through a meadow rimmed by low hills. A river cut sluggishly through the ripened grasses. White-trunked aspens, a few sporting autumn gold, punctuated a hillside covered with the dark green of pine, fir and spruce. The beautiful view was flawed, however, by the man sitting beside her.

"I detest do-gooders who think they know best how to run everyone else's life."

"This is Moraine Park. Those are piles of debris left behind by retreating glaciers centuries before." Adam pointed to the low hills before continuing in the same impersonal tone of voice. "As far as I'm concerned, you could wallow in your self-pity from now until the glaciers come back. However, you happen to possess a skill I have need of. A skill, I might add, I'm willing to pay top dollar for."

"You don't give up, do you?"

"No."

"You needn't sound so pleased with yourself. You're less flexible than those old glaciers. Even they knew when to back off. Let me tell you, Adam Traherne, pig-headed, stiff-necked obstinacy is not an admirable trait."

"And here I was thinking obstinacy is a trait you're well acquainted with."

"You don't think anything of the sort. You think since I caved in and came with you, you can manipulate me into doing anything you want. Guess again, Mr. Hot-Shot Lawyer. I only came because no one, not even a overbearing, interfering busybody like you, is going to say I don't pay my debts. I'll go to this stupid Grizzly Lake—''

"Bear Lake."

"—and then we're even. Neither one of us ever has to cross the other's path again. Now. As long as you've dragged me out here, the least you can do is to tell me about it. Or is little boy thwarted going to sit there and pout?"

"I've never believed in justifiable homicide, but you could make a believer of me."

"Very amusing. Why don't you just admit you don't know a thing about this place?"

"Ladies and gentlemen, I bid you and the reluctant visitor on my right—" he dipped his head in Sunny's direction "—welcome to the 414 square miles known as Rocky Mountain National Park. You are not the first to set foot in this breathtaking gem of the Rockies. Early man undoubtedly viewed these same majestic peaks, hunted these same valleys, traversed these same ridges."

Sunny cut into his singsong delivery. "How come there's no one around? The last time I visited Blythe, we drove through part of the park, and tourists were everywhere."

"Do not interrupt the guide," he said sternly before resuming his spiel. "Some say French fur traders arrived next, others claim a trapper by the name of Sage beat the trappers." The powerful car clung to the sharp, climbing hairpin curves. "That's ignoring, of course, the Ute and Arapaho Indians who'd been coming and going. Joel Estes showed up in the 1860s and tried to raise cattle. He gave up, but his name stuck." Adam pulled into a large parking lot. "In the summer tourists are so

abundant they have to take a shuttle bus to the lake.
We're lucky today. Only two other cars here.''

Sunny stepped from the car and pulled a knit cap down
over her ears. ''If I were truly lucky, I'd be home, instead of freezing to death here.'' She zipped shut her
heavy jacket and trudged up the path in Adam's wake.
Cresting the small incline, she abruptly halted. Directly
in front of them a small lake nestled at the bottom of
dark, pine-covered slopes while in the distance a sheer,
forbidding gray peak cleaved the blue sky. Forgetting
she was here under duress, Sunny drank in the incredible
beauty.

Adam spoke from behind her. ''That sheer cliff is
Hallett Peak. There's an asphalt path around the lake.
It's only about a half-mile long. Come on.'' He strode
off to their right, taking her compliance for granted.

Sunny considered walking in the opposite direction,
but decided doing so would be childish. Not that he gave
her any credit for maturity, she thought as she followed
him along the trail, eyeing his back resentfully. A furious
chattering beside the trail overcame her indignation. A
small gray animal ran down a nearby tree. ''A baby
squirrel. Look how little he is.''

''Not a baby,'' Adam said. ''A chickaree. He's a small
tree squirrel. That's as big as he grows.'' The animal
bounded across the rocky ground and scrambled up to
the top of another tree. ''Emily and I come here often.
She loves the animal life.''

''Emily?''

''My niece. She's almost three. Her idea of a hike is
stopping every six inches to investigate whatever catches
her eye.'' A chipmunk scurried from between two large
boulders and raced across the path in front of them. At
the water's edge the small, striped animal drank, ignoring the presence of humans.

A log bench in the sun beckoned to Sunny. "Emily is your brother's daughter?"

"Yes." Adam dropped down beside Sunny. "She's a blond, brown-eyed angel."

"Who has her uncle wrapped around her finger." Sunny breathed deeply of the scented pine. Chickadees flitted through the trees calling back and forth to each other.

"With her father gone, I try to spend as much time with her as I can. She and her mother are in Brussels right now visiting my parents." He hesitated, then added, "I can't give her back her father or replace him. That's why it's so important you paint her father's portrait."

Sunny looked across the lake. The placid surface of the water mirrored a snow-powdered peak and the nearer darkly forested hills. "What mountain is that?"

"Longs Peak." Adam stretched his legs across the path. "No explosion at my mention of the portrait. Should I conclude you're considering it?"

"No." A small gust of wind ruffled the surface of the dark water, disturbing the peaceful mountain reflections.

"Emily was barely two when her father died. Not old enough to remember him when she grows up. I want her to know what he was like."

"I'm sorry, but I can't help you."

"Christian was easygoing, funny, my best friend. He was a super guy."

"I'm sure he was, but I'm not—"

"My dad's a career diplomat," he continued as though she hadn't spoken. "He and Mom have lived around the globe. Extra duties, for both of them, come with those kinds of jobs. Sometimes they were stationed in the back of beyond. From the time my brother and I were fourteen, we went to boarding school. I was older so my folks expected me to be responsible for Christian. A different kind of kid might have resented me, but not Christian. Not that he was a goody-goody. He got into his share of jams.''

"Which I suppose you got him out of.''

"I never minded looking out for him.''

"And now you're looking out for his daughter.''

"As you would look out for Bud or his brothers.''

"I wouldn't ask you to paint them a stupid picture.'' Her harsh words sent the chipmunk scurrying to a distant rock.

"It would be pointless. I can't paint.''

"Neither can I.'' A charged silence followed Sunny's denial. The chipmunk sat still as a statue high on the boulder overlooking the path.

"Would you care to explain?'' Adam finally asked.

Sunny pushed dried leaves around with the toe of her shoe. Out on the lake a pair of mallard ducks glided near the shore. The male's green head gleamed darkly before he dove beneath the cold water's surface. She shivered.

"After Grumps came home from the hospital the second time, after he'd had the blood clot problem, I didn't have time to write or paint except for silly little pictures and stories to cheer him up. I was making darned sure the blood clots didn't reoccur, so I nagged him and kept him moving and massaged his legs.

"During the nights I set the alarm every few hours and got up and rubbed his legs and made him move around in his bed. After he went back to sleep, I'd lay awake in bed, the doors between our bedrooms open, and I'd listen to his breathing. One of the symptoms of a clot stuck in the lung is coughing, and I'd think I heard him cough and race in to check on him.''

She shrugged. "I stupidly allowed myself to get run down, so it's no surprise I fell prey to the first germ that came along. Since then, I've tried to paint, but..." She looked down at her hands. "There's nothing there."

"It doesn't sound as if there was much there to begin with."

Sunny swallowed an angry denial. There was no defense against the truth. "Do you want to go back or continue around the lake?"

Adam stood up. With a rush of wings and frenzied splashing, the mallards erupted into the sky. "Continue." He pulled her to her feet before striding down the path. "I finish what I begin."

"Aren't you Mr. Wonderful?" Glaring wrathfully at the broad back ahead of her, she stomped through a large patch of snow that lay in the shadows of an enormous boulder. "It must be nice to be so sure of one's self."

"At least I'm honest with myself." He flung the words back over one shoulder. "Your books are works of art. Colorful and lush illustrations. Simple fables, not simple at all, but allegories with multiple layers and textures. That kind of talent doesn't disappear into thin air."

Fir and alder shaded the path, preventing the sun from melting the snow along the silt-filled end of the lake. The combination of tramping feet with warm days and cold nights had turned the snow to slush and ice. Adam skirted a treacherously slick area of the path.

"Either you're lying to me or you're lying to yourself. Or you're a self-pitying weakling. Where would Emily be if her mother and I and her grandparents were all quitters like you?"

"I'm not a quitter!" Sunny bent down and scooped up a handful of snow. Packing it solidly into a ball, she threw the snow as hard as she could at Adam. The snowball exploded in the middle of his back. When he swung around, she yelled, "And even if I was, at least I'm not acting like a big baby because I'm not getting my own way."

He faced her, leg spread wide, hands on his hips. "You certainly like to live dangerously."

"I suppose that's some kind of threat to make me tremble in my boots. I've got news for you, Mr. Know-It-All Lawyer, you may scare every crook in Colorado, but you don't scare me."

"Maybe you think I'm too civilized to retaliate." He took a step in her direction.

She refused to be bullied. "I doubt very much if you have even a nodding acquaintance with civilized behavior."

"I'm acquainted enough to know when other people need to be taught some manners."

"By whom?" Reading the answer to her challenging question on his face, Sunny moved quickly backward. Stepping on an icy spot, her feet flew from beneath her.

Adam caught her before she landed in the cold, wet snow. "You know what they say about the wheels of justice."

Sunny glared defiantly at the dark face so close to hers. "If there were any justice in this world, I would have spent my entire life without running into you. Let go of me."

Fingers bit through layers of coat, squeezing her shoulders as Adam hauled her up on her toes. "You forgot to thank me for saving you from a fall." His grip tightened. "You need a lesson in manners."

"I don't need anything from you." Her defiant gaze locked with his. Staring into his brown eyes, she knew the exact instant when a heated awareness of her as a woman replaced Adam's irritation. A powerful and primitive tension seemed to shimmer between them. "I . . ." She cleared her throat and tried again. "I don't like you."

Adam's eyes turned opaque and unreadable. He stared coolly down at her. "You don't have to like me. Just paint my brother's portrait."

"I can't." Sunny took a deep breath, filling her lungs with the crisp autumn air. "So go away and leave me alone."

"I will." Releasing Sunny's shoulders, he locked one hand around her arm and pulled her along the trail. "As soon as you paint the portrait."

"Forget it." Digging her heels into a patch of snow, she threw her free arm around the nearest tree.

Adam almost jerked off her other arm before he realized what she was doing. "Would you try to act like a reasonable adult?"

"I don't like your definition of reasonable, and since you have problems with that, I suggest we simply pretend we've never met. You probably think your disappearance will break my heart, but I'll survive. Just go away."

"Don't tempt me." He dropped her arm. "It's a hell of a long hike back to your house."

"I'm a hell of a hiker," she said coldly, brushing stray bits of bark from her coat. Did he really think he could coerce her into painting his stupid picture for the sake of a ride back to the house? She'd hitchhike first.

He dogged her footsteps as she marched on around the end of the lake. "You're mad because I didn't kiss you."

"Excuse me? Has the high altitude destroyed your brain or something? Kissing you ranks right up there with running a car over my foot."

"Liar. You know as well as I do there's been a physical attraction between us from the moment I found you nailed to your sister's windowsill."

"While I am, of course, intensely gratified to hear my great beauty devastated you on impact, let me assure you the feeling is not mutual. I'm not attracted to you." Distracted by the unwelcome realization she was lying, Sunny stepped blindly into a drift. The icy snow particles filling her boot did little to calm her. Nor did Adam's next words.

"You needn't flatter yourself I'll curl up and die if I don't get you in my bed."

"We were hardly discussing anyone getting in anyone's bed."

"Not on a conscious level, no."

"Not on any level," she snapped. "I'm not interested."

"Is there a boyfriend back in Omaha?"

Skidding to a halt, she whirled and scowled at him. "That's none of your business."

"Meaning there isn't."

"Whether there is or isn't is beside the point. This may come as a shock to you, but I don't like men who are insensitive boors and who always want to have everything their way."

"I have a feeling you intend for me to include myself in that category."

"I'm not overly optimistic about it."

"You're a strange woman. Sassy, obstinate, foolhardy—"

"I'm not foolhardy."

He stopped in front of another log bench and sat, leaning back on his hands, looking up at her. "What do you call driving clear across Nebraska without food?

Breaking into an empty house? Never locking your doors? Always challenging a man twice your size?''

"I'm sorry." She opened her eyes wide. "Am I supposed to be frightened of you?" For an answer he yanked on her leg, knocking her off balance. She tumbled to the bench beside him. "Let me guess. Now you're going to show me how tough you are. Gosh. It's too bad you're wearing a winter coat or I could feel how big your muscles are."

The only muscle she could see was the one twitching in his cheek. Hopefully it was a sign of intense irritation. Maybe with a little more needling she could annoy him to the point he'd be thrilled if they never crossed paths again. An event, on her part, devoutly wished for.

"Your cheeks are finally getting some color," he said abruptly. "Coming here has been good for you."

Sunny wrapped her arms around her knees. "If you think I'll thank you for this little enforced excursion, forget it." Across the lake the low-riding sun spotlighted the tip and notch of Longs Peak, bathing the snow with a peachy glow. She hugged her legs tightly in the growing chill of the late afternoon. "Fresh air has nothing to do with any roses in my cheeks."

"I didn't say anything about fresh air. Temper tantrums produced those rosy cheeks."

"Don't talk to me about temper tantrums. You're the one pitching a fit because you can't have your way." The mallards were back, swimming slowly, etching ever-widening circles on the smooth surface of the lake. "Is this the way you act in court? Badgering witnesses and bullying the jury? I thought lawyers were supposed to be cool and self-contained."

"When they're fighting for justice. I'm fighting for my family."

"How touching."

"You ought to think so, considering you're claiming you sacrificed health and career for your family."

The sun headed behind the western slopes with a last colorful explosion of color while evening shadows stole across the lake, seeking out with icy fingers the log bench they sat on. A Steller's jay flew in low between the pines. At the last minute, spotting them on the bench, he abruptly changed course and squawked alarms into the darkening sky. All bird song around them stilled.

"I never made any such claim," Sunny finally said. She burrowed deeper into her jacket, shivering in the brooding quiet. "I'm cold. Let's go." Jumping to her feet, she hurried down the path toward the parking lot.

Adam unlocked the car doors and they drove in silence back to town. Dusk had descended, and elk were dark shadows moving into the valleys. Ahead of them a mule deer, caught in the glare of the car headlights, faced them, her large ears pointing to the sky, her entire body alert and cautious. At the last minute she dashed for the woods, her tail held high, her rump flashing white as she bounded over downed trees.

Sunny huddled against the door, envying the doe her easy escape.

Adam brought the car to a halt in his own driveway. "I'd like you to reconsider your answer about doing the portrait."

"No." She reached for the door handle.

His hand closed over her arm. "Christian used to say one of my biggest faults was that I couldn't leave a mystery alone. I had to solve it."

"I'm amazed he could single out one fault." She bolted from the car. "You have so many."

"For example, your refusal to paint the portrait mystifies me." He followed her across the pine-needle-covered ground to her house. "I'm offering you easy money. You don't have to figure out what to paint or change your style. I don't want a formal portrait in oil. I want a picture a child can relate to, the kind of thing you did so well in your books.'' He leaned against the outside wall as Sunny fumbled in her pockets for the house key. "The question is why you're refusing."

"I told you why. I can't." She finally found the key and jammed it in the keyhole.

Reaching around her, he grabbed the edge of the open door, barring her entry into the house. "I have faith in you."

"Faith!'' She heard the hysteria in her voice and swallowed hard. "All the faith in the world isn't going to make any difference. If a person can't, she can't. I don't know if I'll ever write or paint again." She ducked under his arm.

"That's pure bunk, and you know it." He strolled into the hall as if he owned the house. "You can't walk away from a talent like yours."

Sunny flipped a switch, bathing the room in light. "Let me guess. You're not only stubborn and a bully, you're a mind reader, too." Tearing off her jacket, she threw it toward the nearest chair, the zippers clattering against the wood.

"I doubt anyone can read what's going on in what passes for your mind. Were your first books too successful and you're afraid to try again because you might not measure up? No, that's not the problem. You mentioned you were working when you discovered your stepgrandfather coughing up blood." He paused. "That's it, isn't it?" he slowly guessed. "You blame yourself for his blood clot. And to make amends, you're sacrificing your talent on the altar of guilt."

"Sigmund Freud strikes again." Sunny curled up in the nearest overstuffed chair. "Now that you've figured it out, you can quit bothering me."

"Did the old man plant the idea you're to blame?" Adam stood in front of the fireplace, his elbow casually propped on the mantel. "Or did you come up with that inane conclusion all by yourself?"

"It's not inane," Sunny said wearily. "It's the truth. I was so wrapped up in my work... I usually went with him on his daily walk, but that day I was preoccupied with an idea I was working on... I told him I could walk later, but he knew once I got involved, he wouldn't get me out of the studio, so he went without me.

"I didn't hear him go. I didn't even hear the ambulance. And when he came home from the hospital, I failed him again. Worrying more about the stupid book I was working on... Not that Grumps blames me. He's a saint."

"A blind saint if he doesn't see all that nonsense rotting your brain."

"He has no idea... He thinks I've been unable to work because I haven't completely recovered from the flu."

"Does he? Or is he secretly pleased at the notion he has so much power over you? He wouldn't be the first person to exploit a weakness in someone in order to control them. He's the one afraid of your success. He's undoubtedly terrified you'll go off and leave him to endure old age all by himself. You've been babbling on about how close the two of you are, but the truth is, he probably doesn't care at all about you. He's just using you."

The brutal words drove the blood from Sunny's brain. "That's a horrible, cruel thing to say." Rage bubbled up inside her. "Grumps is a better person than you'll

ever be. We may be related only by marriage, but he's
my grandfather in every sense of the word.''

Martin was an only son, and Blythe and Sunny were
the only grandchildren Grumps had. And Blythe was
fourteen years older than Sunny, and already married to
Dillon by the time their mother married Martin. Grumps
had never become the jolly old gentleman of her imagination, but he was her best friend.

''I don't care what you think or say about me,'' she
said, ''but don't you ever, ever again say anything bad
about Grumps. If he had the slightest idea—'' She broke
off, belatedly registering Adam's intense, almost ex-
pectant demeanor. Comprehension slowly dawned. ''Do
you really think,'' she asked evenly, ''outrageous accusations will change my mind?''

He shrugged. ''Not if they're true.''

'''Not if they're true,''' Sunny repeated softly. She
absently smoothed the fabric over the arms of the chair.
''You are incredibly arrogant, but your clever little trick
won't work. You can't bully me, nor am I so easily
manipulated.''

''Manipulated?''

The too innocent voice was a dead giveaway. ''All that
rot about Grumps and me.'' Her voice grew more confident. Adam Traherne wasn't half as smart as he imagined he was. ''You thought I'd jump up and proclaim
that Grumps does love me and is proud of me and wants
me to succeed, and to prove it, I'll paint your stupid
portrait. But I won't.''

''You're telling me I can't bully you and I can't shame
you into doing this book.''

''You can not.'' She didn't bother to hide her triumph.

''Why not?''

''I told you—''

''Everything but the truth. Try it for a change.''

CHAPTER FIVE

TRIUMPH fled. Sunny gripped the arms of the chair, sinking back into its aged depths. The chair had belonged to her mother until a few years ago when she'd given the chair to Blythe who'd reupholstered it for her vacation home. Sunny's favorite refuge as a child, a place she curled up with her favorite doll and felt safe, the chair didn't make her feel safe now. Adam waited.

In an emotionless monotone, Sunny said, "It was Grumps's idea that I make one of my stories into a picture book. Without his encouragement and financial support, I'd probably be teaching art in an elementary school somewhere. He was so proud of me when *The Melancholy Apple Prince* sold. He urged me on to create *The Blue Bird In The Banana Tree*. I couldn't believe it when it sold, too, but he's never doubted my abilities for a minute. He has such faith in me."

She dug her fingernails deep into the padded fabric. "Then he became ill, and, well, one thing led to another and now..." Huddled against the tall chair back, she focused her gaze on an overhead beam. A cobweb showed silver in the room's artificial light.

"You won't believe me, but I have tried to work. When I thought Grumps might die, I thought about things I'd never done, never said. I couldn't bear the idea he might die without knowing how much I loved him, how much I owed him. I determined if he got well, I'd write a book dedicated to him." She scraped her nails along one arm of the chair.

"I've started dozens of projects...all just so much waste paper. You saw my silly little sketches the other day. That's all I'm capable of doing anymore. Painting used to bring me such joy. Now it's a chore. And one I'm no longer good at. It's as if my fingers are no longer mine. I can't paint a book for Grumps." A fly buzzed around the edges of the spider's web. Sunny closed her eyes.

"And I can't paint a portrait for you. Scream at me, call me names, threaten me, point a gun at my head— it doesn't matter. I can't do it."

"I see." He paused. A gust of wind rattled pine branches against a window. "I was wrong earlier, wasn't I?" he asked slowly. "About you sacrificing your talent because you blamed yourself for your stepgrandfather's problems. Guilt has nothing to do with it, does it? We're talking about anger, aren't we?"

Her eyes popped open. "I'm not talking at all. And I haven't the faintest idea what you're talking about."

"Don't you? You thought the old man was going to die. You said you laid awake nights worrying about a blood clot in his lung killing him. You were terrified you'd lose someone you cared very much about. And if he did die and leave you, whose fault would his death have been? Yours? Or his? You told him you'd walk with him later, but he chose not to wait. He knew he was supposed to exercise. If he cared anything about you, he would have taken better care of himself, right?"

"Don't be ridiculous."

"But he didn't take care of himself. So you won't paint another picture or write another book. That'll teach him, right?"

"That's stupid."

"The truth sometimes is. I ought to have seen it from the start. I was angry enough at Christian for getting himself killed."

"Just because you're sick, don't think I am, too." Her fingers were curved talons digging into the chair's fabric.

"Sunny, it's common," he said gently. "Anger comes from fear and pain. All that emotion has to find an outlet. When you stub your toe on a chair, your first reaction is an urge to kick the chair."

"You can't compare a man almost dying to stubbing your toe," Sunny said in outrage.

"The principle is the same. You're hurt, and you want to hurt back. You said your stepgrandfather was proud of you and your books. It's not a long leap to realize the one thing that would hurt him most is you giving up your career because of him. Not that I think you've worked that all out in your mind. Our subconscious can be a pretty powerful force."

Sunny wanted to shriek at him to shut up. Instead she tightly clamped her jaws and said nothing. Closing her eyes, she blotted out the sight of him and concentrated on controlling the fury burning through her body. She was not angry with Grumps. She was not. The clattering of the ice-maker dumping ice cubes in the freezer abruptly broke the silence, startling Sunny into opening her eyes. Adam was still slouched against the fireplace. The sympathetic look on his face was worse than his mockery or accusations. Springing from the chair, she dashed to the back door and threw it open. "Get out and don't come back."

"I need to return to Denver this evening, but I'm due some time off." He ambled toward her. "I'll be back up in a few days after I take care of several items on my desk. You'll need more information about my brother before you start the portrait."

"I am not going to paint the stupid portrait for you."
Sunny tightened her grip on the doorknob. "I can't keep
you from coming to Estes Park, but don't bother to run
over to say hello. Believe me, my doors will definitely
be locked."

"You forget." One corner of his mouth quirked
upward. "I have a key." His lips firmed. "And, Ms.
Taite," he added softly, standing toe to toe with her,
"don't consider ducking out. Tracking you down would
be child's play."

"I'm aware you consider me a total weakling and a
complete nitwit, but I have news for you, Mr. Traherne."
She refused to back away. "I may get myself into ridiculous situations, but I draw the line at being pushed
around by bullies, and I certainly am not going to let a
psychopathic thug like you chase me away from Estes
Park."

The menacing air and using his physical bulk to assert
his domination might work in the courtroom with a
hostile witness, but it wasn't going to succeed with her.
She looked him straight in the eye as he loomed over
her. "After a couple days of mature reflection, you'll
decide another artist will be better for your purposes.
When that happens you needn't worry about apologizing for insulting and hassling me. Never seeing you
again will be sufficient compensation."

"You're wrong. I won't decide I want another artist."
Reaching out, he took hold of the fat braid hanging down
her back and drew the end across her neck. "You're
wrong about something else, too. I don't think you're
a weakling. Putting your life aside to nurse someone back
to health, even someone you care a great deal about, is
no bed of roses. Your succumbing to illness is proof of
how you must have exhausted yourself, but you did it
because the old man needed you."

He pulled the braid snugly under her chin, forcing her head up higher. "I'm wondering if, beneath all the hysterical bleating, you're not a hell of a lot tougher than you make out to be."

Sunny stared at him, torn between outrage and a wild, inexplicable urge to laugh. Only this man would compliment her and insult her in the same sentence. "You can't possibly believe flattery will change my mind."

"I was merely stating the truth." He curved his fingers around her chin. "If I wanted to flatter you," his thumb brushed lightly against her lips, "I'd deny I thought you were a nitwit." He hesitated, looking down at her. "The old man is lucky to have someone like you bringing sunshine into his life," he said softly. "Sunshine and wildflowers and golden honey."

She forgot to breathe. She didn't like this man. Or his dimpled chin. Nature had no right to give a man a dimple that a woman could drown in. The dimple moved closer. Did he really think he could kiss her into compliance? She was no teenager to be swayed by six feet of solid masculinity and rugged, dark good looks.

She licked her dry lips. Adam's hand cradled her chin, and he tipped her head further back. Maybe his eyes did remind her of warm chocolate fudge, and maybe his black hair did make her think of silken threads, but she was past the age of being charmed insensible by sexy, handsome men. Even ones who looked at her with this potent combination of amusement and male awareness.

Sunny lowered her lashes, wary, yet intrigued by the look in dark brown eyes only inches away. Warm breath caressed her skin. Adam's kiss was light and gentle, a brush of lips over her mouth. Fingers grazed her neck, setting the nerve endings in her skin dancing. She sighed, her lips parting on the soft sound.

Adam deepened the kiss for the barest fraction of a second, and then his hands slid to her shoulders and he held her away from him. "See you in a couple of days." A friendly tap on the end of her nose and he was gone.

Sunny shut the door with shaking hands. Half dazed, she wandered over to the window. Wispy white clouds partially covered a crescent moon. Longs Peak was a vague black shadow against a midnight-blue sky pierced with a few lonely stars. Lights sprang on in the house next door casting golden rectangles onto the ground between the houses. Adam's silhouette crossed in front of a shade-covered window. She swept faded draperies across the cold expanse of glass. If only blocking out Adam's words were as easy.

Restless, Sunny picked up a faded cushion from the nearest chair and plumped up the stuffing. Grumps would never be ashamed of her, and she wasn't angry with Grumps. What kind of person got mad at a brother for dying? As if Christian Traherne had any choice in the matter. It wasn't as if he could have gone to a soothsayer and found out death was coming. Or taken better care of himself. Exercised. No, she didn't mean that. Adam Traherne had planted those traitorous thoughts in her brain.

She didn't blame Grumps. She was the one who'd almost killed him. Naturally Adam Traherne wouldn't understand her feelings. He wasn't the type to blame himself for anything. No, Adam Traherne was perfect. Made of unyielding steel, he never made mistakes.

Grumps would understand. If she could discuss it with him, which she couldn't, because he'd feel guilty and blame himself. She was surprised he hadn't already figured out what was going on in her head. Of course, he had been ill and that did tend to concentrate one's thoughts on oneself. Not that she wanted Grumps worrying about her. She just wanted...

Sunny slammed the pillow to the floor and kicked it across the room. She wasn't angry with Grumps. Darn Adam Traherne. It was his fault. Pushing and shoving at her. Messing with her mind. Confusing her.

"Don't be blaming someone else for your faults."

The words echoed so clearly in the empty room Sunny almost turned to look for Grumps. "Come on, Grumps, you're in Omaha," she grumbled out loud. "Your orders were that I'm not supposed to call you, write you, ask about you, worry about you or even think about you, remember? I'm just supposed to rest and recuperate. So don't be haunting me. I don't need you or Mr. Hot-Shot Lawyer acting as my conscience." She didn't need Adam Traherne for anything.

Including kisses. Sunny traced her mouth with the balls of her fingers. Warm lips pressed against hers were merely another example of Adam Traherne's reprehensible willingness to go to any length to get his own way. They were no reason for her legs to feel as if they were made of gelatin.

For several days, the uncomfortable suspicion persisted that Adam Traherne might be correct about Grumps being ashamed of her. Not because he'd think she was a coward or a quitter, but because he'd think she wasn't trying hard enough to shake off the lingering after-effects of her exhaustion and illness. He certainly wouldn't accuse her of refusing to work to punish him. Only Adam Traherne would say a horrid thing like that. And Adam Traherne was capable of saying anything in order to get his own way. He was certainly wrong about her being angry with Grumps.

The only thing he'd been right about from the moment she'd laid eyes on him was that she ought to have locked her doors. And even that appeared more and more unnecessary.

By Thursday, Sunny was convinced Adam Traherne's threat to return had been mere bombast. Of course, she'd never been worried about caving in to his demand. Walking out on the deck, Sunny took a deep breath of mountain air. Life without Adam Traherne was simply less objectionable. Propping her forearms on the deck railing, she lifted her face to the autumn sun.

At the far end of the deck two greedy evening grosbeaks gobbled up sunflower seeds from the platform feeder. The sharp snap of a branch breaking startled the birds into flight. Sunny froze. She had company. It wasn't necessary to turn around to know who was coming.

"Still here, I see." Adam climbed the half dozen steps to the deck.

She closed her eyes, the sun's heat beating down on her skin. "Did you think I wouldn't be?"

"I was sure you would be." He leaned on the railing beside her. "I brought you a few things. Pictures of my brother and some very crude sketches to show you what I have in mind."

A splinter dug into her skin. As if she needed a reminder that Adam Traherne was a big pain. An intermittent breeze carried the scent of his soap to her. Sunny kept her eyes closed. Maybe if she refused to look at him, he'd disappear. "I thought mosquito season was over."

"Mosquito season?"

"The time of year when irritating, pesky bugs buzz and buzz and buzz until a person finally gets annoyed enough to swat them." She paused for effect. "Dead."

"I've heard only the female mosquito draws blood." His voice was tinged with amusement.

"Meaning the male is irritating but impotent?"

He laughed, clearly unstung, and opened her back door. "Let's discuss this inside."

She remained stationary. "I'm not interested."

The door clicking shut was her only answer. She knew he was perfectly capable of dragging her in from the deck. Stopping a runaway locomotive would be a cinch compared to stopping Adam Traherne. He had to be the most arrogant, obstinate, single-minded person she'd ever met. He'd decided he wanted a portrait of his brother done by Sunny Taite and little obstacles such as Sunny Taite didn't want to paint the portrait or Sunny Taite was no longer capable of painting such a portrait were totally irrelevant to him.

Obviously what Adam Traherne wanted, he was accustomed to getting. Not this time. Best to confront him and be done with it.

For a few more seconds she soaked up the peaceful afternoon, the warmth of the sun, the bird songs, the scent of pine. Then, with a deep sigh, she turned to go inside.

Adam must have come directly from his office. This was the first time she'd seen him in anything other than casual clothes. If his shoulders looked broader and his chest wider, credit the dark charcoal pinstripe business suit which conveyed subtle messages of power and strength. Reassuring to clients and intimidating to foes, Sunny thought. What she didn't understand was how a man dressed so conservatively could look so overwhelmingly and dangerously male. Unless it was the hint of beard darkening his lower face or the lazy brown eyes that watched her enter.

Sitting on the sofa, he leaned back, loosening his tie. A large box sat on the low table in front of him along with a sheaf of papers. "I wrote up a contract. You'll want to read it carefully.'' He pulled a pen from his breast pocket and uncapped it. "I think you'll find I've covered the essentials in a manner fair and equitable to us both."

Slowly Sunny reached out her hand and accepted the papers he handed her. Just as slowly she shredded the contract into tiny bits, the white fragments floating to the hardwood floor in a blizzard of paper. Finished, she brushed her hands together, scrunched down into the nearest easy chair, and glared at him. "Give it up!" she said crossly. "You're starting to bore me."

"I'd like you to look at the photographs I brought."

"No." When his eyes narrowed at her bald refusal, she added, "There's no point in looking. I won't change my mind. I'm not going to paint your brother's portrait."

He stared appraisingly at her, a slight frown puckering his forehead. Minutes ticked by, the sun arcing to the west. Finally he seemed to reach a decision and slowly uncoiled his body from the low sofa. "All right." His lips curved, exposing strong white teeth. If it was a smile, it failed to reach his eyes. "As you pointed out earlier, there are other artists." He held out his hand. "No hard feelings?"

Sunny looked from the outstretched hand to his face. If Adam Traherne felt the least bit contrite about his reprehensible behavior toward her, no trace of remorse evidenced itself. His dark brown eyes studied her intently, and she had the sense he was deliberately tamping down an emotion she couldn't quite decipher. The uneasy suspicion that he was waiting for something took root in her mind.

Suddenly Sunny felt very cold. Adam Traherne was not giving up. No matter what he said, his surrender was at best a strategic retreat to allow him to gain some advantage over her. Slowly she put her hands behind her back. The brown eyes changed fractionally, reminding

her of a beagle she'd once had who'd looked at her with
that same mournful expression when she'd yelled at him
for chewing up her shoes. Not for one instant did she
believe in the sincerity of his expression. "I want to forget
the whole thing," she said.

"Of course." A faint smile, tinged with understanding and regret, played at the edges of his mouth.

He was acting. She knew he was acting. She barely
restrained herself from grabbing his arm and asking him
what game he was playing as he went out the back door.
He made no attempt to steal another goodbye kiss. Not
that she wanted him to. Sunny sagged against the closed
door. Maybe she was wrong. Maybe Adam had conceded. He'd drive back to Denver and any future meet-
ings between them would be purely accidental. She could
forget Adam Traherne had ever intruded in her life.

Taking a deep breath, Sunny inhaled the lingering scent
of Adam's after-shave. And wondered why being left
alone no longer held for her the appeal it had held last
week.

Pushing away from the door, she noticed the white
paper scraps still littering the floor and stooped to pick
them up. The large, flat box on the low coffee table
caught her eye. Adam had forgotten his box. She reached
out with her hand and then drew back.

Instinctively Sunny knew opening the box would be
akin to opening Pandora's box. Every brain cell she possessed screamed Adam had not left the box accidentally.
She doubted Adam ever did anything accidentally. Her
suspicion that Adam yielded too easily resurfaced. Obviously the box contained photographs of his brother.
And just as obviously, he'd deliberately left the photographs. The only question was why.

The answer came immediately. He wanted her to look
in the box. There was something about the photographs

which he believed would change her mind about painting the portrait. He was wrong. Nothing in the box could change her mind. Not that she was going to look. The entire box was going in the garbage, contents sight unseen.

Reaching for it, Sunny stopped. Trashing the box wasn't the answer. Even stomping outside and dumping the box in Adam's garbage can failed to do justice to her feelings. This cute little trick was absolutely the last straw. It was time Mr. Hot-Shot Lawyer learned, once and for all, no matter what he did, he was not going to get his way. He was not going to get a portrait by Sunny Taite.

Wrenching open the glass doors to the fireplace, Sunny crammed crumpled newspapers into the dark cavern and lit a match. Heavy black smoke billowed up inside the fireplace. She shoved more paper into the blazing fire, determined to keep the conflagration going until Adam noticed the smoke pouring from the chimney.

The black smoke would send him running, and the second he burst through her back door, she intended to toss the entire box of photos into the blazing fireplace. The flames crackled and snapped, the column of heat and smoke lifting huge black cinders up the chimney piece. Sunny fed more and more crumpled newspaper into the ravenous fire.

The heat blasting from the open fireplace drove her back toward the sofa. The box on the table, so innocent-looking, drew her eye. It wouldn't hurt to take one tiny peek inside. Sunny sat down on the sofa and stared at the box, reaching out tentatively with one hand only to snatch the hand back. Coward, an inner voice jeered, if you're so positive there's nothing in the box to change your mind, what are you afraid of? Nothing, she told herself firmly, grabbing the box and hastily tearing off the lid. Dropping the box in her lap, Sunny stared down at the top photograph.

The back door burst open and crashed against the wall. Adam raced across the floor, dropping to his knees in front of the fireplace. "Damn you," he said bleakly. With a loud crackle, the last newspaper disintegrated into a small pile of burning embers. The flames died out, and the remaining dark cinders spiraled lazily upward. "Damn you. I'd like to wring your neck."

"Why not?" Sunny asked bitterly. "That's about the only thing you haven't done to me since I arrived."

"Nothing I've done deserves you burning those photographs." He rose stiffly to his feet, the muscles of his back taut with anger. "I thought if you saw the bond between them . . ." he said almost to himself.

"Your brother looks like you. Was he another selfish, bullying steamroller who totally disregarded other peoples' feelings when he wanted something?"

Adam stilled, then turned slowly, a comprehensive glance taking in her and the open box on her lap. "You opened it."

"Didn't you know I would?"

"It was a gamble. I thought I'd lost when I saw the smoke."

"Leaving them was a dirty trick." Sunny held up the uppermost photograph. "How long did it take you to decide this one should be on top?"

"I thought about it awhile," he said cautiously.

She inelegantly wiped her nose on the back of her hand. "It's such a stupid picture. How old was your niece?"

"Less than two."

"Why in the world did she have the string of that balloon between her teeth?"

"She was playing with it, and when it got stuck, she wouldn't let Christian remove it. They went through the entire shopping mall with the balloon flying over Emily's head. Joanna said when they returned home and she saw them, she laughed so hard she could hardly take the picture."

"It's the looks on their faces," Sunny said. "Even as young as she is, she's aware she's done something quite clever. Not because it is, but because your brother thinks so. He's laughing, yet absolutely delighted with her."

"Christian was crazy about Emily." Adam sat down across from her, a watchful expression on his face. "I want a portrait that will show her that."

"And whatever Adam wants..." she said sharply. "It would have served you right if I'd burned the photographs."

"It never occurred to me you might destroy them."

"And if they didn't work, what next? Seduction? Were all those stupid kisses meant to soften me up just in case?"

"Would seduction have worked?"

"No." Carrying the box over to the dining table, Sunny spread the pictures over the wooden surface. Emily was a photogenic toddler of many moods, her soft brown eyes dominating a sweet face framed with wispy blond hair. The sheer number of photographs attested to how loved the toddler was. A hollow ache settled in Sunny's middle, and the small pixie face in the photographs blurred.

"I should never have told you my father died when I was young." She outlined the child's face with her finger. "He wasn't tall, but he was a broad man. When he came home from work, he'd whistle and I'd come running and grab his hands and walk up his bent legs and twist my legs around his stomach and then he'd let go, and I'd throw my arms around his neck and he'd hug me.

"My mother talks about trips we took and a birdhouse we built, but I don't remember those. Sometimes I have trouble remembering what he looks like, but I'll always remember climbing up him. And the way we laughed when he hugged me." She grabbed a tissue from the box on the kitchen countertop and blew her nose.

"I should have shown you the photographs earlier," Adam said. "That cute, prickly exterior of yours hides a marshmallow heart."

Sunny bristled. "Don't gloat." She continued to shift through the photographs. "I haven't said I'd paint the portrait. You're a toad, and if your brother was anything like you, he probably was, too."

"If something had happened to me and I'd left behind a wife and child, Christian would have cared for them to the best of his ability. If taking care of a dead brother's family is your definition of a toad," Adam said levelly, "then, yes, Christian and I would both plead guilty to being toads."

"I suppose it's not Emily's fault she got stuck with you for an uncle. But if I do it, it will be for her, not you." Deep inside her, Sunny knew what she had to do. Emily was so young to have already learned one of the harshest lessons of life.

"If you do it, I don't give a damn why you do it."

After a long silence, Sunny held up a photograph from the pile. "Your brother's wife?"

Adam moved to her side. "Yes, that's Joanna."

"She's beautiful. I see where Emily got her hair." A critical eye might have found the blond woman's mouth too wide, but Sunny saw no other flaw in the blue-eyed, confident beauty smiling up from the table. The woman was elegant and drop-dead gorgeous in a way Sunny could never hope to be. "Your brother must have loved her very much."

"They seemed to get along OK."

"'Get along,'" she repeated in disgust. She shuffled the pictures. "Look at this photo, and the way he's looking at her. Any idiot can see they were deeply in love. Were you jealous of her? Did she come between you and your brother? Is that why you won't admit he loved her?"

"I was not jealous of Joanna. As for my brother loving his wife, he said he did." Adam shrugged. "I'm not convinced love between a man and a woman is possible, but obviously I don't have your extensive experience."

"A person doesn't have to fall in love to believe in it. I've been around Blythe and Dillon and Mom and Martin enough to know love is a very wonderful and powerful force." She absently traced around the edges of a photo. "Love is caring passionately about another's well-being, rooms lighting up when someone special walks in, bells ringing when he kisses you."

"How many bells have you heard?" His voice was heavy with sarcasm.

"I'll hear them. When I meet a man and fall in love with him in spite of his flaws and scars and wrinkles and imperfections, then I'll know he's the right man for me. I'll hear the bells, and I'll know it's true love."

"Bells. True love. Hell, you're about as wise as Emily. True love's a fantasy for children and fools. Spend a couple of days in court listening to divorce and custody cases."

Adam moved across the room to stand at the window, one long arm bracing himself against the frame, his back to her. "I don't take on divorce cases, but my partners handle some. If you saw the way people who were sup-posedly madly in love at one time turn on each other with hatred and anger... Their children become pawns in the cruelest, most vicious game invented by mankind—custody." His voice resonated with loathing. "If there were such a thing as love, it wouldn't be about hurting and destroying and winning at any cost."

"Not all marriages are like that. Maybe those people weren't ever really in love."

"And maybe you aren't the expert on love and marriage you think you are. Joanna and Christian were a well-balanced couple with common backgrounds, interests and goals. Sensible people go into marriage with their eyes open, not with the unrealistic expectations of a fairy-tale romance."

"If you believe that, I feel sorry for you."

Adam snorted derisively, turning to rest one hip on the windowsill. "Listen to who's feeling sorry for me. A newly hatched chick. I'm only thirty-two, but those grayish-blue eyes of yours shine with such innocence, you make me feel I'm a hundred years old. You don't have a clue what life is about."

"Don't I?" The photographs blurred before her unseeing eyes. "Life is your father dying, your mother remarrying a wonderful man, but a man in the military so you're uprooted and hauled all over the country. Life can be very lonely, especially when you're terrified another special person is going to be taken from you." She forced the last words over the lump in her throat. "I know all about life."

"Maybe you have had some rough times, but you're still a dewy-eyed optimist. You're the type who believes in a pot of gold at the end of every rainbow."

"I know what's real and what's illusion. I know life can be cruel and unfair. And I know love can hurt, but you have to risk it."

"You're a great one to be talking about risk."

The mocking words stung. "It must be difficult being the only flawless person in a weak and flawed world." Sunny pressed her fingers painfully hard against the tabletop and took a deep breath. "If you want me to paint your brother, you'll have to refrain from constantly attacking me."

"Are you going to paint the portrait?"

She chewed her bottom lip. "I don't know," she said shakily. "I'm going to try." When he didn't answer she glared across the room. "And if it's a disaster, don't blame me. You could have found someone else."

"I didn't want someone else." He strolled back to the table. "Let me show you some photos I particularly like. I have a pretty good idea how I want the portrait painted."

"Fine. Go home and paint it. In the meantime, leave me alone. A person can't order up a painting the way you order up a hamburger. I'll decide what I'm going to paint."

"Wait a minute. I'm paying you—"

"The money's not important," she interrupted impatiently. "If you like the portrait when I'm finished, fine. Ten thousand is too much, but I can always use the money. The painting will be for Emily. A celebration of the love between her and her father."

"While I appreciate—"

"I don't want your appreciation. I want peace and quiet so I can think. Go home."

Hours later, Sunny tossed down her sketchbook and stretched aching muscles. Her stomach reminded her the dinner hour had come and gone. There was a hot dog buried in the freezer, and she dumped it in a pan of water to boil on the stove.

Thumbnail sketches littered the tabletop. Some were a few hastily drawn lines, others more filled in, but none were intricately drawn. These were preliminary drawings, done to get down on paper some of the ideas jostling around in her brain. Later would come detailed roughs and full-size sketches.

Reviewing her evening's efforts, Sunny felt the tiniest lifting of her spirits. She'd forgotten the excitement and anticipation stemming from embarking upon a new project. Even the ache of muscles was a satisfying ache. She bit into her hot dog, absently wiping mustard from her chin as the mortifying thought struck her that Adam might have been right about her.

Had she abandoned her work to punish herself because she blamed herself for Grumps's accident? Even worse was the idea that subconsciously she wanted to be a failure to punish Grumps for not waiting for her to go for his walk. He wouldn't have torn up his knee if she'd been along. And if he hadn't been such a wimp about his pain and exercised his leg the way he was supposed to... Darn Adam Traherne for planting such wicked thoughts. Both of them wrong, dead wrong.

Her eyes burned. There was no getting around the fact that Grumps was bothered by the way she'd neglected her work. He'd specifically hired Esther in order for Sunny to return to her studio. He'd claimed Sunny's hovering was driving him crazy, but she knew he was concerned about all the excuses she'd given for not working. He just didn't understand how much he'd frightened her. She hadn't realized how she'd repressed all her feelings about losing her father until she'd come close to losing Grumps.

A glimmer of an idea danced at the edges of her brain. She and Emily weren't the only children to lose a loved one to death. People tended to overlook children's grief and suffering, but their pain was real. As were their fears and bewilderment. The right sort of book could address these feelings, not as a cure, but as a shared understanding. She didn't know if she was capable of creating such a book, but as Grumps was fond of reminding her, she wouldn't know until she tried. Dear Grumps. He was going to be elated when he learned she was working again.

Night had fallen and through the uncurtained windows, lights glowed from the tall house next door. Sunny sipped from a can of pop. The single-minded, selfish bully who lived there needn't give himself any credit because her urge to work had returned. Adam Traherne didn't possess any special insight or understanding. He would have warned her that not painting would cause her hands to fall off if he thought it would get him what he wanted.

Slipping into her nightshirt later, Sunny mentally explored the drawbacks inherent in agreeing to paint the portrait of Christian Traherne. It was inevitable her ideas would clash with Adam's. Visualizing him hanging over her, criticizing and suggesting and interfering, and generally driving her berserk, she fell asleep in the midst of plotting various nefarious schemes, all designed to rid herself of the pest next door.

With morning, the question of how to make Adam disappear was no closer to being answered. At least he hadn't appeared on her doorstep laden with turkey sausage. Sipping her coffee, Sunny shuffled the photographs spread across the dining table. Her attention was caught by one of Emily riding her father's shoulders in a swimming pool as they played some kind of game with Adam. Adam was holding up a large ball, the water streaming down his sinewy arms and muscular chest.

Sunny swallowed a bite of doughnut, an outrageous idea taking shape in her mind. Adam Traherne probably knew less about drawing than she knew about pleading a case in court. Put that lack of knowledge together with his obsession about Sunny painting his brother...

Sunny smiled with unholy glee. Adam Traherne had done enough blabbering yesterday about their cooperating on the portrait. She knew exactly what his idea of cooperation entailed. Her doing his bidding. It might be interesting to see if Adam Traherne was prepared to cooperate in other ways. Somehow she doubted it.

Her smile turned into a grin. By noon she'd have him running back to Denver with his tail tucked between his legs. She went straight to the phone. Dillon had insisted on giving her Adam's phone number. In case of trouble, he'd said. There was more than one kind of trouble.

CHAPTER SIX

"YOU must be joking!"

At Adam's outraged shout, Sunny held the receiver away from her ear. Although it was probably too late for her eardrum. "If you don't want to..." She let the words trail off. "I thought you wanted me to do my best."

"What you're suggesting is ridiculous and hardly necessary. Work from the photographs."

"I didn't realize you wanted calendar art," she said dismissively, "but if you don't mind your brother looking like a wooden, two-dimensional stick figure..."

"It's November. I don't have a bathing suit with me."

"I'm sure you can find one in one of the stores downtown. Estes Park is a resort town." She winced as the phone at the other end of the line was slammed down.

If she was any judge of character, Adam would be calling back in about thirty minutes to tell her there wasn't a single bathing suit to be purchased in all of Estes Park. Then she'd suggest he could model nude, and about that time he'd remember urgent business in Denver. In case he decided to make his excuses in person, she quickly sketched a few rough, lifeless outlines.

It was closer to an hour before Adam marched through her back door after a cursory knock. The look on his face was as black as the sweatshirt and pants Sunny was not surprised to see him wearing. Swallowing her laughter, she gravely inspected him, slowly shaking her head.

97

"Those clothes completely obscure the figure. I need to be able to see muscle structure and body mass, or your brother's portrait won't have any movement. It will be static, lifeless." She wouldn't have thought it possible for the look on his face to turn any blacker.

"It's not exactly sun-tanning weather out there." Yanking at the ties at his waist, he stripped the sweatpants from his legs and tossed them on the nearest chair. His sweatshirt quickly followed. "I don't want to hear any smart-aleck remarks," he said through gritted teeth. "It was the only one I could find that came close to fitting."

Sunny blinked at the scrap of psychedelic fabric hugging his hips. She should have realized Adam would totally screw up her plan. He wasn't supposed to consent to pose. Luckily she'd discarded her initial idea of suggesting he pose in the nude, or he might be standing in front of her without a stitch on. Which was the last thing she wanted.

Adam might be the usual muscles and bones and skin, but unfortunately for Sunny's peace of mind, nature had fashioned those common components into an uncommonly sensual male figure. Adam Traherne was solid but there wasn't an ounce of fat on him. It shouldn't have come as any surprise that a man with such dark hair and a constant five-o'clock shadow would also have legs and arms sprinkled with dark hairs. Not that his arms and legs interested her in the least. It was the sexy mat of chest hair she found so distracting. Her scheme was definitely not working as designed.

"Quit trying to think of something polite to say. I know I look ridiculous. Let's get this over with."

Thank goodness the man had flunked mind-reading. "You need to relax, loosen up. I can't draw you when you're all tense." He wasn't the only tense one.

"You'd be tense, too, if you were wearing nothing more than a wide neon bandage."

"You needn't be embarrassed. We frequently used nude models in drawing class. An artist's only concern is getting a figure's proportions correct or using the right colorwash for skin tones." Certainly in those classes her mind hadn't dwelt on wondering how it would feel to run her fingers through the curly hairs on a male chest. Unsure whom she was trying to convince, she added, "You're nothing more than a bowl of apples to me."

"How reassuring."

The dry comment reminded Sunny of Adam's reputation for astuteness. Cautiously she proceeded with her plan, circling him, tapping her pencil against her bottom lip, her face, she hoped, a mask of intense concentration. The chilly room air contracted his nipples into hard points.

Niggling doubts about the wisdom of her scheme poked at her, but Sunny resolutely ignored them. "Stand here, sideways to the window, in the sunlight. Widen your stance, not that much, and rest your hands on your hips." His shoulders were broad; his chest tapered to a narrow waist. She moved across the room and gazed at him in deliberation. "Let your hands hang down naturally."

"There's nothing natural about any of this."

Sunny couldn't agree more. It certainly wasn't natural for a man to have thighs like tree trunks and not look totally muscle-bound or fat. Adam Traherne was definitely neither. Even worse, he had the kind of tight bottom teenage girls swooned over. Only she wasn't a teenage girl. She was a sane and sensible adult, too old to be mentally drooling over some hot-shot lawyer because he had a body designed for action movies.

It was time to apply more pressure and escalate the ouster-Adam campaign. He shifted his weight, causing corded muscles to ripple in his well-shaped upper arms. "You have to stand still," she said sharply.

He scowled at her. "If you think this is so easy, trade places with me."

"If you could draw, you wouldn't need me." She handed him a pillow. "Hold this up in the air. It's Emily," she answered his unspoken question. "She and your brother are in the pool." Her hands on his smooth shoulders, Sunny twisted his sinewy upper torso, her palms gliding slowly over his skin as she experimented with various poses. The heat from his body singed her skin.

She cleared her throat. "There. Now turn your head." She ran her fingers lightly over the black silken cap of hair that followed the contours of his head. "Like this." Standing back, Sunny caught her breath. The tableau she'd created was designed to express paternal devotion and adoration, but in spite of the pillow and ridiculous swimming suit, the inner confidence and serene masculinity radiating from Adam Traherne endowed the scene with provocatively sensual overtones.

Resolutely ignoring a small quiver running through her middle regions, Sunny filled a large glass with tap water from the kitchen. She walked around him, frowning as she muttered about the light. "Turn—" she manipulated his shoulders "—like so. I want to check the effect of the sunlight." She poured some water down his back.

He jumped as if electrically shocked. "What the hell?"

"Water. You're supposed to be in a swimming pool, remember?" She viewed his back with disfavor. "You shook off all the water."

"Was it necessary to use ice water?"

"Don't be such a baby. You're supposed to be in a pool, not a hot tub. Turn around." She rained more water over his shoulders and down his chest.

Adam heroically limited his reaction to a few choice swear words. Droplets of water clung to the hair on his chest. His nipples pointed straight at Sunny. "Must you strive for total authenticity?"

"You want my best efforts, don't you?" Biting her lower lip in a pose of total absorption in her task, Sunny studied him for a long moment before dipping her hand in the glass. Dribbling water down his chest again, she artistically spread the liquid over his skin and rearranged the dark curly hairs. His chest hairs were softer than they looked and several curled around her fingers. The water was cold, but his skin was warm.

Wetting her thumb in the glass, she carefully deposited one drop of water above Adam's left nipple. The clear liquid bead slowly rolled down his chest until it caught on the small, hard tip. Just before the droplet fell off, Sunny caught it with her thumb and slowly pushed it back up his chest, her thumb catching momentarily as it moved across the pointed nub.

Once again, she released the tiny bead to begin its downward journey, once again catching it an infinitesimal moment before it splashed to the floor. Her thumb brushed his nipple.

The pillow fell to the floor with a loud thunk. A large solid hand closed around Sunny's fingers, pressing them against his warm chest. "Having fun?"

"This isn't about fun," Sunny said. The tips of her fingers burned. "It's about striving for accuracy."

"Is it?" he questioned softly. "Or did you have something else entirely in mind?"

"Such as what?" She attempted to wrench her hand free.

He tightened his grip. "You tell me."

"There's nothing to tell." Maintaining innocence in the face of Adam's penetrating gaze proved surprisingly difficult, and Sunny dropped her eyes. A mistake of maximum dimensions, as her view was composed mainly of dark, curly masculine hairs and one firm male nipple.

Taking a deep breath proved another mistake. His scent was disturbingly male. More bedroom than courtroom. Not an image to dwell upon. She forced her thoughts to the issue at hand. Getting rid of this man.

"You're certainly making a big deal out of nothing." She shrugged. "I didn't realize you suffered from hydrophobia. That's a fear of water," she added in a kindly voice.

Adam appropriated the glass and set it on the windowsill. "What I suffer from is a fear of nitwits who don't have the sense to realize they're engaging in extremely provocative behavior."

"I'm not a nitwit."

"No? You intend the provocation? That puts a whole new complexion on your behavior, doesn't it? I'm the nitwit—" grasping her other hand, he corraled both in the small of her back "—not to have realized when you insisted I come over here half nude that you were planning a little neighborly seduction."

"I was not. You seem to think every woman who so much as breathes the same air as you is dying to leap into your bed."

His arms were holding her much too close to him. His bare shins tempted her to kick him. Except she'd probably break a toe if the rest of him was as thick as his head.

"Let me assure you," she said, "any seductive behavior you're ascribing to me exists entirely in your overactive imagination."

"Then tell me what this is about, and I don't want to hear any nonsense about authenticity. If you weren't trying to seduce me..." His grip tightened. "You obviously have some scheme in mind."

Any explanation that didn't touch on the truth eluded her. "Only an egotistical moron like you would think I'm the least bit attracted to you."

"I may be an egotistical moron, but I'm bright enough to notice you offer no other explanation for your behavior."

"Only the truth," she lied, glaring up at him.

"There's a stiff penalty for perjury. Any lawyer would advise you to tell the truth on the witness stand."

"I'm not on the witness stand." She stared fixedly at his nose. Noses were safe. They weren't hot-chocolate warm with amusement as some people's eyes were. Nor were they as lethal as masculine lips above a devastating dimple. "And I didn't ask you for any advice. I doubt I could afford your fee."

"My fees are open to negotiation." He lowered his head.

"I'll remember that," she managed to say, "if I ever get in trouble."

"Honey, you're already in trouble," he said softly, the last words spoken against her mouth.

He outweighed her or she would have fought him. Plus, if she stepped on his toes and broke one, he'd undoubtedly sue her. Everybody knew lawyers were good at that. She closed her eyes to blot out his disturbing gaze. Blotting out the scent and feel of him proved impossible. Large hard fists in her back pressed her length against his firm body, flattening her breasts against his muscled chest. Two layers of clothing failed to insulate her from the heat blazing from his bare skin.

His mouth was hot and demanding, and her lips parted. Irritation at a masculine sound of satisfaction was rapidly dispelled by the unexpected pleasures spiraling through her midsection. She'd draw back in a minute. After satisfying a certain feminine curiosity.

Wiggling her arms free from Adam's confining grip, Sunny wound them around his neck. He lowered his hands to cup her hips, and her body softened and melted into his steel embrace. He murmured his approval as he abandoned her mouth to rain kisses across the sensitive skin of her cheek, her jaw, her earlobe. Tipping back her head, he pressed his mouth against the blood wildly pulsing at the base of her throat. She clutched at his shoulders, her ears filled with the sounds of a million drums.

"If sleeping with your model is how you get to know the inner man," Adam said, his words muffled against Sunny's throat, "I'm ready to give my all for the sake of true art."

The amusement in his voice penetrated before the words did. Sunny blinked, then broke free of his embrace. "Very funny. If you don't want to cooperate, just say so."

Adam allowed her to move two steps before his hand clamped on her arm, abruptly halting her. "I am willing to cooperate. Didn't I make myself clear?"

"That's not the type of cooperation I meant, and you know it." She glared at the large hand locked on her wrist.

"I know pouring water on me had nothing to do with the portrait."

"Then you know nothing, brilliant, all-knowing, hot-shot lawyer that you are," she mocked. "Your brain is as muscle-bound as your body. And I haven't the slightest interest in either." His raised eyebrows, eloquent of disbelief, goaded her into adding, "You can't think I enjoy being mauled by you. When I'm working, I concentrate totally on what I'm doing. Naturally, your attack took me by surprise."

"Naturally."

She frowned at his bland tone. "It wasn't necessary to attack me. I suppose I should have realized your co-operation had its limits, but it never occurred to me that a big, bad man like you would be terrified of a few drops of water."

His fingers slid up her arm to firmly cup her elbow. "What did you think a big, bad man like me would be terrified of? A puny little female pipsqueak acting out a bad seduction scene?" He ignored her indignant gasp. "Honey, more experienced women than you have used their far lusher bodies in an attempt to influence me. I recognize a con game when I see one."

His other hand curled around her throat, his thumb forcing her face up toward his. "And the first rule when attempting a con, is to know your target." The tips of his fingers gently massaged her neck. "Thoroughly."

"Stop it." His disparaging comparisons about experience and female bodies rankled. "Flexing your muscles and spouting male menace won't frighten me. Why are you trying to intimidate me? I'm doing what you want."

He released her, crossing his arms in front of his bare chest. "You're not doing the portrait because of anything I did or said. You're doing it for your own private reasons, whatever they may be."

Sunny removed the water glass from the windowsill and carried it to the kitchen, dumping the water into the sink and setting the glass on the countertop. "Why do I have the impression you've actually convinced yourself you're doing me a favor by bullying me into doing the portrait?"

"Truthfully," he drawled, "I believe I *am* doing you a favor."

Whirling, she stared at him in disbelief. "Oh-hh, you're, you're... Success in the courtroom has gone to your head. Well, Mr. Hot-Shot Attorney, maybe you can twist facts around and make black appear white to gullible jurors who believe every priceless gem dripping from your silver tongue, but I can see past good looks and a stupid cleft chin to the truth."

"I question whether truth is a concept you have any acquaintance with whatsoever."

"I haven't lied to you. I told you from the beginning I didn't want to do the stupid portrait."

"I'm not talking about the portrait. I'm talking about the lie you've been living."

"I haven't the faintest idea what you're babbling about," Sunny said coldly.

"Be honest with yourself. It's not that you couldn't paint anymore. The truth is you quit painting. The only questions are whether you're trying to punish yourself or punish the old man. And whether you'll actually paint a portrait of my brother, or just make a few halfhearted stabs at it and then whine that you can't do it."

"I told you I'd try." Sunny leaned back against the counter, her hands behind her clutching the edge of the stainless-steel sink. "I don't know why you keep saying such hurtful things."

"Somebody has to say them. Everyone else is too busy feeling sorry for you. They can't see what's going on." He frowned thoughtfully at her. "Maybe the truth is you've been having a damned good time, wallowing in an orgy of self-pity, setting yourself up as the family martyr. And your family is obliging you by buying into the whole illusion. St. Sunny the Martyr. Yeah, you hang on to that image.'' He strolled toward her.

"It's a pretty cozy little deception. Your family making excuses for you, worried sick about you, lending you homes, wiping your nose... Hell, they'd probably be willing to support you the rest of your life. You'd never have to work again.''

"You are the most despicable excuse for a human being I've ever met,'' Sunny said in a low, fierce voice. Her fingers curled tightly around the handle of a skillet soaking in the sink. "I detest you.''

Adam gave a short, barking laugh. "No, you hate me seeing the truth. You foolishly fell into the trap of believing your own pathetic little excuses. Then I came along and forced you to take a good look at yourself, and you didn't like what you saw. Poor Sunny,'' he said, his voice laced with mock sympathy.

Humiliated and furious at his contemptuous assessment of her, Sunny erupted, swinging the contents of the skillet at Adam. The cold, greasy water hit him chest level. The pan had been used for frying eggs and bacon for her breakfast, and yellow scraps of yolk clung to his chest hairs while brown rivulets ran down his skin and soaked into the bathing suit. Grease formed shiny circles around browned bacon bits; the stains did nothing to improve the stridently colored fabric.

An ominous silence filled the room as Adam contemplated the damage. "I can't decide whether it would be more satisfying to sue the socks off you,'' he said, "or to bang you over the head with that damned pan.''

"Don't you touch me.'' Sunny pressed against the cabinet and tightened her backhanded grip on the skillet, wielding the pan as if it were a tennis racket. "I've got a black belt in karate.'' Inwardly she cursed a temperament that had once again jet-propelled her into disaster.

Adam jerked the skillet from her hands and slammed it down on the countertop. Reaching out, he grabbed Sunny's shirt, his dark gaze locked with hers, daring her to struggle. There was no mistaking the anger gleaming dark and deep within predatory eyes. Reading the grim intent on his face, she froze, fear racing through her veins.

Adam gave a grunt of satisfaction. Slowly he twisted the knit shirt around his fingers until the fabric strained around her shoulders, inexorably drawing her to within millimeters of his dripping body. His rock-hard fist dug into her middle. Sunny felt the blood drain from her head while a keen sense of self-preservation held her silent.

"Dry," he commanded.

"What?"

"Dry me off. And don't miss a drop, or I'll make you lick it off."

"You wouldn't dare," she breathed.

"Don't—tempt—me," he said, hammering out the words from between clenched teeth.

Sunny reached behind her for the kitchen towel.

"No." Adam delivered a stinging slap to her wrist. "Use your shirt."

Sunny instantly took exception to the order. "I am not—"

"You are," he said with soft menace, tightening his grip on her shirt to haul her up on her toes. "Now. Before I decide anyone behaving so childishly should be punished as a child."

Sunny stared into the unblinking eyes inches from her face and decided only a fool would challenge a man who was obviously looking for an excuse to explode. Nor did she harbor any curiosity about his notion of punishment suitable for children. Although she doubted if standing in the corner was on his mind.

"All right." Taking the hem of her shirt, she swiped at Adam's midriff. "But I'm not going to apologize. My behavior may have been rash, even childish," she quickly added as his muscles twitched, "but ever since I arrived here, you've been putting me down and calling me names, and I'm sick and tired of it.

"I'm not a martyr, but I never pretended to be a heroine, either. I had to deal with a family emergency and I've been ill. Now I'm tired and depressed, and if that makes me a weakling, I don't care. We can't all be unemotional machines that never break down."

His chest wasn't clean, but it was dry. Biting the corner of her lower lip, she took a deep breath and reached toward the waistband of his bathing suit.

Adam grabbed her hand. "I think the swimsuit is best cleaned without me in it." Surveying the puddle on the floor, he added, "I want two bath towels. I'll take a shower while you clean this up. Then we'll talk."

It came as no surprise that Adam Traherne was too pigheaded to admit he was in any way at fault. However, there were times to hold ground and times to retreat and regroup. Sunny tamely followed Adam down the hall. The towels were in a closet outside the bathroom. She handed him two.

"I hope you like perfumed soap." The bathroom door slammed in her face. "You'd think a hot-shot lawyer could afford indoor plumbing in his house," she shouted, emboldened by the solid wooden door between them. From inside the bathroom came the sound of water gushing from the shower.

Muttering, Sunny retraced her steps to the kitchen and set about cleaning up the mess. Maybe her behavior was infantile. Certainly Blythe's sophisticated eyebrows would climb to the ceiling if she saw her baby sister tossing dirty dishwater in a man's face. Not that this particular man didn't deserve it. He was lucky he hadn't received the skillet smack across his sanctimonious mouth.

Sunny rinsed the cleaning rag under the faucet, ignoring the howl of rage echoing down the hall. Water pressure had always been a problem in this house. Flushing toilets subjected showerers to boiling hot water, while running hot water in the kitchen sent ice cold water cascading from the shower head.

She turned off the water. After a brief wait to ensure Adam had readjusted the shower temperature, she turned the hot water on again full force. Adam Traherne could use some cooling off. Another howl ripped from the bathroom. What a baby he was. On the heels of that thought came the disconcerting awareness that he wasn't the only baby around. Sunny swiftly turned off the water, shamed by her childish behavior. Mopping the last evidence of her tantrum from the floor, she sincerely hoped Adam Traherne was too civilized to commit murder.

She also hoped this latest evidence of their inability to get along would convince him to return to Denver. Leaving the photographs behind. To work, she needed peace. Sunny wrung out the rag. Even if Adam departed, peace would be pretty elusive. It didn't take a genius to realize her anger derived not from Adam hurling accusations, but from a fear he might be right. Everyone said she'd coped magnificently with Grumps's accident, knee surgery and pulmonary embolism. It wasn't until he'd recovered that she'd admitted to herself how close she'd come to losing him and how terrified she'd been at the thought of his death.

Outwardly, she'd remained calm and cheerful. Inwardly she'd gone totally to pieces. The strain had been horrendous. No wonder she'd become ill herself. An illness that had lingered and evolved into a black cloud of depression.

Maybe if she could have talked to someone, but Grumps was her best friend and she could hardly discuss her confused thoughts and fears with him. So she'd continued to bottle up everything within her, using her illness as a refuge and excuse rather than facing up to feelings she didn't want to acknowledge.

Grumps had scared her spitless. He could have waited for her to go on his walk. There. She admitted it. She was angry, really angry at him for scaring her so badly. She hung the rag over the sink to dry, straightening the sides and taking care the corners matched. The anger had produced guilt, and a combination of the two made her question her own sanity and moral center. What kind of person raged at an old man for almost dying?

Adam admitted he'd been angry at his brother for dying. Sunny had been too young to fully comprehend the finality of death when her father was killed. Now she wondered if her mother had been angry. And Blythe. They'd never discussed the death of their father. Had Blythe been angry and felt abandoned?

Sunny wiped moisture from one cheek. That Adam Traherne might be right was a disagreeable thought. She hated people who were right. At least he'd been sidetracked from delving into why she'd persuaded him to pose.

She'd been an idiot to think her little scheme would succeed in chasing Adam away. If she'd been patient, in a day or two he would have grown bored with the process of painting the portrait and returned to his other interests. Unfortunately, patience had never been one of her strengths. The first time they'd met Adam had called her a nitwit, and Sunny was humiliatingly aware she'd in no way proved otherwise.

She changed her shirt and wandered aimlessly about the great room until her gaze fell upon her sketchbook and pencil. Retrieving her materials, Sunny curled up in one of the overstuffed chairs. Maybe sketching would clear her mind and refocus her thoughts. The scratching of pencil across paper curiously comforted her, and she quickly lost herself in her drawing.

The sound of a car scattering gravel barely penetrated her concentration, until familiar voices dragged her abruptly back to awareness. Looking out the window, she caught a fleeting glimpse of a passing elbow. A familiar luxury car sat in the drive.

A key scratched in the front lock and two whirling dervishes catapulted through the doorway. "Surprise!" the twins yelled in unison.

"Surprise," Sunny echoed weakly, looking over her nephews' heads at their brother and mother following closely behind. "What are you doing here?"

Blythe tossed her purse on the nearest chair and shrugged out of her jacket. "We've come to take you back to Denver. I talked to Mom and Nolan, and we all agree you'll be better off in Denver with us."

"Thanks, Blythe." Sunny emerged from the ritualized greeting tussle with Daniel and David. "But I'd rather stay here." She welcomed Bud with a fond punch on his arm. "Tell Mom and Nolan not to worry. I'm doing fine."

"Nolan says you weren't eating." Blythe enveloped Sunny in a warm, perfumed hug. "In Denver I can see that you eat right and get the proper amount of sleep and exercise. Besides, Dillon just hired the nicest man—"

"He's a geek," David said.

"A major geek," Daniel added.

"He is not. He's intelligent, clever and—"

"A real nerd," Bud interrupted his mother. "Mom's gotta be desperate to trot him out."

"You boys keep quiet. You don't know what you're talking about. Besides, Sunny has higher standards than you do. Now, let's get your things," Blythe said briskly to Sunny. "I've invited Walter to dinner this weekend, but you needn't feel obliged to go out with him or anything."

"Walter?"

"I just told you," Blythe said impatiently. "The new man in Dillon's office."

"Oh," Sunny said, "the dweeb."

"Nah," Bud said. "Old Walter's a nerd."

"A geek," David and Daniel added in unison.

"Boys," their mother cast a minatory eye on them.

"I can't come," Sunny said. Solemnly she added, "I didn't pack a thing to wear suitable for meeting a geek or a nerd. Sorry." She winked at her nephews.

Blythe ignored her sons' snickering. "We'll go shopping."

"Blythe. You're not listening. Thanks for the invitation, but I'm staying here," Sunny said firmly.

"Why?"

Sunny rolled her eyes. Her sister the steamroller. "I'm working on a project. For which I need peace and quiet." She warded off her sister's next remark. "Don't even say it. You know very well the last place anyone could find peace and quiet is in that zoo your family inhabits."

One of the twins loosed a long wolf whistle. "Gosh, Sunny, I thought you drew kid stuff."

Sunny whirled. Her fourteen-year-old nephews were leafing avidly through her sketchbook. "Give me that," she said sharply.

Dealing with three sons had long ago honed Blythe's instincts for scenting something suspicious. She snatched the sketchbook from David's grasp a millisecond before Sunny could grab it. Her eyes widened as she scanned the open page. Slamming the sketchbook on the table, Blythe glared at her younger sister. "What is the meaning of this?"

"Meaning of what?" The innocent inquiry wouldn't fool Blythe for a second. Sunny knew exactly what her sister was referring to. The page Blythe had seen featured thumbnail sketches of Adam's legs, thighs, arms and chest. All had one thing in common. They'd been rendered in a style totally unsuitable for children's books. Sunny forced herself to look squarely at Blythe. "I was scribbling. You know how I do when I'm working out a new idea."

"Heaven only knows what kind of idea you have in mind," Blythe retorted. "Bud, put that down."

"C'mon, Mom. I'm sixteen. What's the big deal? They're just drawings of—"

"Of ideas, and they're private." Sunny grabbed the sketchbook.

Blythe stared thoughtfully at Sunny before turning to her eldest son. "Drawings of whom?"

"Damn it, Sunny, I'm going to wring your neck."

CHAPTER SEVEN

ADAM'S bellowing voice preceded him down the hall. "That business in the shower was..." His mouth snapped shut as he caught sight of his fascinated audience.

Sunny took one look at him and wished a crack in the floor would open and swallow her up. The skimpy bath towel slung low around Adam's waist barely covered his more interesting parts. That realization apparently struck Adam at the same moment, and he hastily lowered the other towel he'd been using to dry his chest. A rivulet of water ran slowly down his flat, muscled abdomen, disappearing into the white terrycloth. Behind him, damp footprints trailed down the hall.

Swallowing a nervous giggle, Sunny looked at her sister. Blythe's face was a study in stunned disbelief.

"I told Mom Sunny wouldn't want to go to Denver." Bud plunged into the thunderous silence.

"Business in the shower?" Blythe asked coldly.

"Go to Denver?" Adam asked at the same moment.

Blythe overrode his question. "What kind of business could you possibly be transacting in the shower?"

Adam was looking at Bud. "What do you mean, go to Denver?"

"Mom wants to fix Sunny up with this Walter nerd."

"Geek," the twins chorused.

Blythe turned on her sons. "To the car. Now!" she shouted as the twins opened their mouths. The boys trudged reluctantly toward the front door.

Ignoring Blythe and her sons, Adam gave Sunny a steady look. "You're not going to Denver."

He was standing in the middle of the house practically stark naked, leading her sister to jump to all kinds of erroneous and stupid conclusions, and that's all he could think about? "You could have at least put on some clothes before you came parading out here," Sunny snapped at him.

"I could have." Adam's gaze traveled across the room to where his black sweatshirt and sweatpants lay heaped on the floor. Blythe's head swiveled in the same direction.

Sunny sighed inwardly. Great. Further proof to bolster Blythe's already-out-of-control suspicions.

"I asked," Blythe said tenaciously, "what kind of business you could possibly be transacting in the shower. And furthermore, what is the meaning of that?" She pointed at the sketchbook Sunny held clutched to her middle. "I want to know what's been going on up here?"

"If anything's going on, and I'm not saying it is, it's none of your business, is it?" Nonchalantly ignoring his unclothed state, Adam leaned against the doorjamb, his dark hair gleaming wetly.

Sunny could have slapped him. Thumbing one's nose at Blythe had much the same effect as throwing kerosene on a roaring fire. "Nothing's going on except I'm working," she said hastily.

Blythe barely acknowledged Sunny's presence, her attention focused on Adam. "You're Adam Traherne," she said. "I didn't recognize you at first."

"Without my clothes, you mean." The slow smile he gave Blythe was bound to infuriate her.

Sunny spoke quickly. "It's not what you're thinking."

"You don't know what I'm thinking," Blythe said curtly, not switching her gaze from Adam. "As for you—" Her nostrils flared in anger. "In spite of the fact you've always behaved in an ill-tempered, uncivilized, boorish manner, I've tried to be neighborly.

"I invited you into my home, invited you to partake of my hospitality, and this is how you repay me? It wasn't enough you made it clear you considered yourself too good for us. It wasn't enough you hate children and have harassed mine from the minute we bought this place. No, you had to seduce my sister!"

"Blythe, quit acting like a character out of a bad play."

"Sunny Taite." Blythe rounded on her. "How could you? In my house!"

"Now wait a minute," Adam said.

"No, you wait a minute," Blythe said. "What kind of man takes advantage of a woman when she's ill and exhausted?"

Sunny tried again. "Blythe, would you please calm down a minute and listen?"

"I would expect such behavior from the likes of him, but you!" Blythe wasn't to be stopped. "Now I know where Bud gets his ideas. No wonder you didn't bother to call me when he showed up in Estes Park," she said bitterly. "You were probably too busy carrying on." She waved in Adam's direction. "With him."

"I think we ought to drop this right now," Sunny said.

Adam shrugged. "Fine with me."

"It's not fine with me," Blythe snapped. "I want to know what's going on in my house."

"Nothing," Sunny said flatly. Blythe's outraged older-sister act had lost its charm. "Leave it be, Blythe."

"While you're in my house, I'm responsible for you."

"I'm twenty-five and responsible for myself. You're not my mother. You have three sons. Worry about them."

"I suppose that's your subtle way of accusing me of being an unfit mother because Bud got drunk and came up here. No doubt he and Jennifer knew they'd fit right in with the kind of debauchery you've been practicing."

Sunny's stomach heaved. "You can't believe—"

"That's enough, Mrs. Reece," Adam said. "You don't merit an explanation of the relationship between Sunny and me. You're merely venting your spleen because you think I've interfered with some nebulous plan you'd conceived with this Walter. Quite frankly, I find you an ill-tempered shrew with a dirty mind. If you were any kind of sister, you'd know Sunny well enough to know she's done nothing that needs explaining."

Blythe glared across the room at Adam. "If you knew anything at all about Sunny, you'd know she doesn't always think things out before she acts."

"You mean she should have thought out what caring for your stepfather's father would entail? She thoughtlessly set aside her career and sacrificed her health, and for what? A man who wasn't even related to her. I notice you weren't dumb enough to leave your fancy Denver home or give up your society parties. It's a damned shame Sunny couldn't be more like you."

"Adam, don't," Sunny said in a low warning voice as a movement beyond the room caught her eye. Bud, disobeying his mother's orders, had stationed himself in the shadowed hallway, out of his mother's view.

Blythe's face wore a pinched, white look. "I know Sunny—"

"You know nothing about Sunny," Adam interrupted. "If you did, you'd thank her for taking in and caring for your drunken son and his equally inebriated girlfriend instead of accusing her of leading them astray."

"I'm not accusing her." Blythe stood her ground. "I'm accusing you."

"Mom!" Bursting in from the hallway, Bud practically jumped up and down in his eagerness to set the record straight. "You've got it all wrong about Sunny and Mr. Traherne. At breakfast the next morning, he—"

"Breakfast," Blythe repeated, staring incredulously at her son. "Your aunt had a man staying overnight with her and you didn't bother to mention it to me?"

"Jeez, Mom, I knew what you'd think. Mr. Traherne practically told me they weren't sleeping together. Sunny isn't his mistress or anything like that."

"Mistress..." Blythe practically strangled over the word. "You discussed it with him?"

"Why not?" Sunny asked. "Isn't that what we're discussing right now?"

"We are not... Bud, I told you to go wait in the car. We'll discuss your behavior later, young man." Blythe waited until the front door slammed shut before squaring off again in front of Sunny. "I want you to pack right this instant. You're going back to Denver with me."

"No, I'm not," Sunny said with equal firmness.

"You're not staying here." Blythe triumphantly played her trump card. "This is my house and I have the final say in who stays here."

"You're kicking me out?" Sunny asked in disbelief.

"Mother would never forgive me for leaving you here in a situation like this."

"There is no situation 'like this'," Sunny said.

"I'll be happy to help you pack," Blythe said in her best grande dame manner. She added, with a regal sniff in Adam's direction, "I'm sure you can manage your clothes on your own, Mr. Traherne."

Adam paid no heed to Blythe, his attention focused on Sunny. She had no difficulty reading his thoughts. "I'll take the materials with me to Omaha and finish up there," she said. "Give me your phone numbers, and if I have any questions I'll call you, here or at your Denver house."

"Omaha is too far away. Move next door into my place."

Sunny slowly shook her head. "I don't think that's a good idea." Beside her, Blythe sputtered with outrage.

He gave her a crooked smile. "Thinking like your sister?"

"It's not a question of not trusting you..."

"Then it's a question of not trusting yourself. Is that what this is all about?" He nodded toward Blythe. "Did you think you needed reinforcements and send for the cavalry?"

"Don't be silly." Sunny made a face. "This is hardly my idea of John Wayne leading troops to the rescue. The point is, I can't work with anyone hanging around, breathing over my shoulder. I could take the photographs with me."

"No. The photographs stay." His smile grew more lopsided. "If you plan to continue, you'll stay, too."

"Why won't you let me take the photos? Don't you trust me?"

He lifted an eyebrow. "Have you given me reason to?"

She couldn't honestly say she had. But moving into the house of a man she barely knew bordered on insanely rash. Yet, Adam wouldn't trust her with the photographs, and without them, she couldn't paint the portrait. The perfect excuse. She could pack up and be back in Omaha by the next night.

Except... She didn't like Adam, but in all fairness she had to admit he was at least partially responsible for the fact that for the first time in weeks her future held more than bleakness and the sure promise of failure. His actions, undertaken for whatever reason, had somehow resurrected the spark of creativity she'd feared was extinguished forever. She owed him.

And there was Emily... Images of the brown-eyed pixie with the string of a balloon caught between her teeth danced before Sunny. Emily's need was Sunny's compulsion. The unalterable truth was as plain as the irritation on Blythe's face. Sunny had to paint the portrait for Emily. And for that she needed Adam's photographs. Only there had to be a solution other than moving into his house. Sunny's troubled gaze met Adam's steady one. "I need the photographs to paint the portrait."

"She is not moving into that house with you. I forbid it, so you can just go away and never bother her again."

Sunny looked at her older sister. "I don't believe I've given you the right to make my decisions for me."

"Don't get on your high horse with me, Sunny Taite. I used to change your diapers. You'll thank me tomorrow for getting you out of this mess."

Sunny's mouth clamped closed on words she'd later regret. Instead she turned to Adam. "It will take me a minute to throw my things together."

Naturally, it wasn't that simple. While Sunny packed, Blythe alternately threatened and cajoled, even going so far as to phone their mother and Nolan. Sunny admitted to a sense of relief when neither were home. By the time Sunny walked out the door, a black-clad Adam carrying her largest suitcase, Blythe was practically foaming at the mouth and working herself into a frenzied attack of hysterics.

Passing Blythe's car, Sunny halted abruptly at the sight of her three nephews staring bug-eyed at her.

Adam strode over to the car, and Bud rolled down the window. "Your mother is a little upset right now," Adam said. "I think it's best Sunny give her a little time to cool off."

After a moment he added, "You don't need to worry about your aunt. I'm not going to harm her in any way. This is strictly a business arrangement. Trust me and trust her, OK?" Three heads bobbed solemnly up and down.

Apparently satisfied with their reactions, Adam said, "Your dad has my phone number. Call Sunny anytime."

Flashing an apologetic smile at the boys, Sunny followed Adam across the yard to his house. "Thank you."

Adam grunted acknowledgment and then was silent as he led her into his house and up the staircase to a spare bedroom. Depositing her bag on the floor, he disappeared down the hall, to return with empty hangers. Conscious of his steady gaze upon her, Sunny slowly unpacked, arranging her clothes on the hangers with deliberate care, all the while berating herself for once again rushing headlong into a situation. Crown her the queen of rash decisions.

If she'd stopped in Denver at Blythe's house there, as planned, she wouldn't be at this minute unpacking her clothes in a stranger's house merely to defy her sister. What kind of idiot was she?

"Second thoughts?" Adam sat on the bed, his hands clasped about one knee.

"Of course not," Sunny lied.

"I meant what I said to your nephews. I'm not going to steal into your bedroom in the dead of night and attack you."

"I never thought you were." She shut the last drawer and shoved her suitcases into the closet. That wasn't a lie. Far more worrisome was this constant, niggling awareness of him.

He stood back, allowing her to exit the room ahead of him. The doorway was narrow, necessitating her brushing against him in passing. A current of electricity surged through her at the unsettling smell of her soap clinging to his skin. She groped for an innocuous remark. "You have a nice house."

"I'm surprised you came."

"I couldn't let Blythe dictate to me." The wooden banister was smooth beneath her palm as Sunny descended the staircase. "Blythe shouldn't have jumped to the conclusion she did."

"The evidence was stacked against you."

"There are lots of reasons you could have been in my shower. Maybe your hot water heater broke down, or your water pipes froze, or...or something."

"And my clothing in the living room?"

"I could have been mending it, or painting on it. I've painted on sweatshirts before."

Adam gave her a dry look. "While their owners cavorted naked through the living room?" Without waiting for an answer, he continued, "I'm starving. Do smoked turkey sandwiches interest you?" He disappeared into the open refrigerator.

If she told him she wanted a cheeseburger and a chocolate shake, he'd probably have apoplexy, Sunny thought, walking across an earth-tone Navaho rug on the wooden floor.

The large room obviously served as living room, dining room and kitchen with furniture arrangements defining the individual functions. Over the sitting area the ceiling rose two stories, the soaring walls fitted with expansive areas of glass in geometric shapes framing the familiar view of Longs Peak. Walls and ceiling were gray-stained cedar with sharp angles and corners creating a play of interesting shadows across the wood. Massive, well-worn black leather chairs faced a gray river-rock fireplace that soared to the high ceiling. A dark red Navaho Indian rug hung above the log mantel.

Floor-to-ceiling, wooden bookcases lining the walls
drew her to them. A jumbled mixture of books, framed
photographs, and personal memorabilia filled the
shelves. A photograph of Adam with the governor of
Colorado brought back snippets of her phone conversation with Dillon concerning Adam Traherne.

After only two years in the prosecutor's office, Adam
had been invited to join one of the most prestigious law
firms in Denver, and was already a partner. Hard work,
with attention to detail and an almost fanatical insistence on providing every client with the best possible
legal advice explained why clients around the nation now
sought out Adam Traherne. Sunny had no trouble believing Adam was single-minded in his work.

Not that being single-minded was such a virtue. If
Adam Traherne wasn't so single-minded about doing
something for his niece, he wouldn't have posed for
Sunny and set into motion events that led to Blythe seeing
him half-naked in her house. A person would think a
hot-shot lawyer would have had more self-respect and
dignity than to pose in a bathing suit. No other man of
her acquaintance would have been crazy enough to pose
for her this morning under the same circumstances.

Crazy enough . . . or selfless enough, a perverse little
voice in her head pointed out. An enlarged photograph
of Adam and Emily pressing their noses together,
laughing, caught Sunny's eye. The love uncle and niece
shared was obvious. The child's face shone with trust
and her brown eyes sparkled with happiness.

"Lunch is ready." Adam stood beside the table. Two
plates heaped with mixed fruit and sandwiches waited.
Sunny sat where he indicated. Sitting across from her,
Adam picked up his napkin, shook open the folds and
placed the paper square on his lap. "Now . . ." Elbows
on the table, he tented his hands over his plate and fo-

cused on Sunny's face. "Where were we when your family so rudely interrupted?"

Sunny squashed her sandwich between her fingers. Deliberately misinterpreting Adam's question, she said lightly, "You were in the shower, and I was scrubbing the kitchen floor."

"Uh-uh. Those activities merely constituted a hiatus in the proceedings."

"Oh. You mean posing."

"That's right. Posing." He bit into a crisp apple and chewed slowly. "There's something strange about that posing. While I was showering, the more I thought about it, the odder I found it."

"Since it bothers you so much," she said airily, "we may as well discontinue it." Only a fool would repeat the mistake of thinking she could scare him away with such dangerous tactics. "I can manage without you."

"Can you?" He studied her over the rim of his water glass. "Then why was my posing so important earlier?" His eyes narrowed. "Maybe it had less to do with the portrait and more to do with a little game of revenge. I maneuvered you into doing something you didn't want to do, so you childishly decided to get back at me by drowning me."

Sunny pulled the crust from her bread. "Don't be ridiculous. How could I have known you'd be so skittish about a couple of drops of water?" She met his gaze across the table. "If I wanted revenge, I could have come up with a better plan than sprinkling a little water on you."

"Your insistence on my posing was obviously calculated to steer me into some course of action, but your motive and goal elude me."

"Quit thinking so much." Sunny toyed with an orange slice. "You'll give yourself a headache."

"If anyone gives me a headache, it'll be you."

"If I'm so bad for your health, go back to Denver."

"Yes, you'd like..." A slow grin crawled across his face. "Yes, you would like that. I am stupid today. You were trying to scare me the hell out of town. I should have been suspicious the minute you mentioned the bathing suit. I was supposed to object to posing, thus giving you an excuse not to paint the portrait."

"I don't know what you're talking about." She shredded the orange slice.

"You know exactly what I'm talking about. You looked a little startled when I unveiled that psychedelic horror, but I attributed your astonishment to a shared sense of disbelief that such a garment actually existed.

"Somewhat belatedly I realize you never expected me to agree to your outrageous demand. You thought I'd hightail it back to Denver and you'd be rid of me. When that didn't work, you threw in a little seduction to terrorize me into running as far from you as I could. You little fool, didn't it occur to you I might accept your invitation?"

"I didn't invite you to do anything but pose."

"You invited me to do more than that."

Sunny felt warm color flood her face. "Just because I kissed you, doesn't mean I'm attracted to you or anything." She carefully used her napkin to wipe sticky orange residue from her fingers. "I don't like you, and I don't like kissing you."

"You don't like the idea of it. The kisses you liked just fine. I wasn't kissing an unresponsive block of wood."

After a moment, Sunny said, "It didn't mean anything."

"I know that. What's between us is nothing more than good, old-fashioned sexual attraction."

"I'm not attracted to you."

He smiled wryly at her vehement denial. "I realize in your fairy-tale version of life, men and women fall in love, then they kiss and finally they go to bed together. I have news for you, Sunny, people constantly tumble in and out of bed together, and love has nothing to do with it."

"Dysfunctional people. Unhappy people."

Adam lifted an eyebrow. "Thus speaks the voice of experience."

"And what makes you the expert on love and marriage?"

"I have marriage plans."

A queer stab of pain sliced through Sunny at Adam's clipped announcement. Dillon hadn't mentioned Adam was dating any particular woman. All he'd said was Adam was an infrequent participant in Denver's social scene, but when he did venture out, usually for a charity function, the woman he escorted was sure to be beautiful and intelligent. Not that it mattered to Sunny if Adam had a dozen fiancées. She was merely surprised.

"I can picture the future Mrs. Lawyer. Beautiful and about eighteen so you can train her in obedience and adoration." She tilted her head, appraising him. "It's difficult, however, to imagine you passionately in love."

"Then don't."

"Funny. I could have sworn you mentioned marriage plans."

"I believe the arrangements call for a June wedding."

"You're joking. No groom sounds so impersonal and uninvolved about his own wedding."

"I'm hardly the blushing bridegroom type."

"For her sake, I hope your bride knows that."

"Rid yourself of the antiquated notion that my future wife is head-over-heels in love with me."

"I suppose she's marrying you for your money. And the prestige she'll gain as Mrs. Adam Traherne."

"She is marrying me because, for a number of reasons, none of which are any of your damned business, our marriage is the logical course of action. Marriage to each other will suit us. We have the same goals, the same interests, the same background. We'll be very comfortable together."

"Marriage isn't about comfort. It's about love and passion—"

"I'm tired of your pronouncements on a subject you know absolutely nothing about. I'm a normal man with normal male urges, and my future wife is a beautiful woman. I don't anticipate any problem with passion," Adam said evenly.

"You've been chasing me around the kitchen table since we met and you haven't taken your fiancée to bed yet?" Sunny asked incredulously.

"There is more to my relationship with my fiancée than tumbling beneath the bed sheets."

Sunny ignored the strange hollow feeling invading her stomach. "That sounds highly moral, but I suspect the truth is, you're so dull and stodgy, your fiancée isn't any too anxious to join you under those bed sheets. And no wonder," she scoffed, pushing back her chair and standing up, "if the most romantic spot you can come up with is that."

"Where would you recommend?" he asked in a mocking voice. "The kitchen floor?"

Carrying her half-eaten sandwich to the sink, she said over her shoulder, "I've always thought fresh air is so healthy. Lying on the ground, one could appreciate the fine tracery of veins in the underside of oak leaves, the way the sun paints dappled patterns on tree trunks and lawn. And at night, the stars, twinkling friendly and cheerful."

Gaining momentum, she further embellished, "The friendly sound of honeybees and crickets, robins calling to their young, the heady perfume of climbing roses, the scent of crushed grass..." She sighed loudly. "Much more romantic than boring bedrooms."

"Don't you think it's a little chilly for you to be cavorting naked through the tulips?"

Sunny stacked her dishes in the dishwasher. "We were discussing ways you could romance your fiancée, not my dating habits. I have no intentions of cavorting naked anywhere." She carefully closed the dishwasher. "Your tulips are safe from me."

"They're certainly safe as far as I'm concerned." Adam carried his dishes to the sink. As Sunny turned to walk away, he caught her arm, lightly encircling her wrist with his fingers.

"While I'm willing to admit the idea of hustling you upstairs into my bedroom has immense appeal, I made a promise to your nephews, and I'll keep my word." Amusement warmed his brown eyes. "The thought of them seeking me out to avenge some imagined injury to their favorite aunt is enough to make any sane man behave." His grip tightened as she attempted to pull away. "So I hope my tulips really are safe from you."

Sunny jerked her arm free. "What is that supposed to mean?"

"I want to know why you really came? And don't give me that garbage about defying your sister. You could have driven back to Omaha and washed your hands of me and the portrait, and there wouldn't have been a thing I could have done about it. So why are you here?"

"Not because I have secret designs on your body." She wasn't about to mention any sense of obligation because that would be tantamount to admitting Adam had been right about her. The implacable look on his face made it clear he wasn't dropping the question until he received an answer that satisfied him.

She'd never met anyone so single-minded in her entire life. "I'm staying because I want to paint the portrait," she finally said. "Are you happy now? I've admitted it. I want to paint the portrait." She spaced the words out for emphasis.

"A rather remarkable change of heart, isn't it?"

"People can change their minds." After a moment she added somberly, "What can't be changed is Emily losing her father."

"In other words, you're staying for Emily's sake."

"Yes. And I would appreciate it if you would back off, keep your opinions to yourself, and allow me to work in peace."

He raised a mocking brow. "Maybe we should draw up a list of rules."

"Fine with me. We can start with no mauling allowed."

"Are you sure you can keep your hands off of me?"

Standing at the window, Sunny watched the six deer bedded down at the edge of the yard. It was almost impossible to distinguish the antlers on two large bucks from the surrounding bare tree branches and stalks of mullein. As she watched, one of the large bucks rose majestically to his feet and strolled toward a stand of trees. Not the slightest signal seemed to pass between him and the others, but they all stood and moved slowly after him. Obviously even animals had a social structure.

Everybody needed somebody. The thought came from nowhere, a thought that should have occurred to her earlier. These odd feelings Adam aroused in her were inexplicable, bothersome and inconvenient. That didn't mean they had anything at all to do with sexual attraction.

Admittedly, he reeked of sex appeal. Blame that on the darned dimple bisecting his chin. And brown eyes shouldn't be allowed to smile so appealingly. Crinkles around eyes were nothing more than wrinkles, and when people said wrinkles were devastating, they were definitely not speaking in a positive sense. No matter what Adam Traherne intimated, he wasn't some god at whose feet she worshiped.

The more she considered the matter, when viewed objectively, her reaction to Adam made perfect sense when one added up all the facts. Her father had died while she was young. Since then she'd always been attracted to older men. She'd practically worshiped Dillon from the moment she'd met him, she adored Martin, her stepfather, and she and Grumps shared a special bond.

The embarrassing truth was that Adam was merely another in a long line of father figures. Relief swept over Sunny. She was certainly not falling in love with him. If wild butterflies rampaged through her stomach when Adam was in the same room, well, she admitted living in his house made her nervous. Adam had been a perfect gentleman, but there was no denying, father figure or not, Adam was a large, sexy, virile male.

"Working hard?"

That a man so large could move so quietly surprised as well as irritated Sunny. "I thought we agreed cracking the whip stifled creativity."

"We haven't agreed on anything since I caught you nailed to the window."

"We agree on that statement," Sunny retorted. "Why are you playing hooky?"

"Now look who's cracking the whip." Walking to the refrigerator, Adam extracted a pitcher. "I've spent the past two hours on the phone trying to convince a willfully deaf client the worst thing he can do is lie to his lawyer." He poured orange juice into a large glass. "I'm dry."

The movements of his throat as he drank deeply caught Sunny's gaze. Esophagus, she told herself. There was nothing attractive about an esophagus. Or the uvula. It was a ridiculous pendulous thing hanging down. And tonsils. Tonsils were . . .

She realized Adam had stopped drinking and was staring curiously at her. She rushed into speech. "I suppose you bullied him into agreeing with you."

"The only thing we agreed on is that another lawyer might serve him better." He set his empty glass on the countertop. "Since we're both playing hooky, grab your coat. I've got a special treat for you."

Sunny was still trying to coax their destination from Adam as he drove his powerful sports car past the motels and tourist attractions bordering the highway. "Are you as arbitrary and as big a bully back in Denver?" she asked in a disgruntled voice. "Or do you come up to Estes and turn into Mountain Jim Nugent?"

"Mountain Jim? Oh, yes, the fierce old character who lived near Estes Park back in the 1870s. Everyone considered him quite a desperado."

"Not everyone. What about Isabella Bird?"

"I suppose you read her book." Adam turned the car onto Elkhorn Avenue, and the distinctive aromas of popcorn and chocolate wafted in through his partially opened window.

"It was on your shelf. You said I could read your books."

"I might have known you'd select a book written by a fanciful romantic."

"Isabella wasn't a fanciful romantic," Sunny said.

"Isabella was an unmarried English woman and Mountain Jim an irascible, gun-toting ruffian with a mysterious past. Just the sort of man fanciful romantics are attracted to."

"It was more than that. I think they fell madly in love. Mountain Jim was supposed to be a bloodthirsty desperado, but he probably had more romance in his little finger than you have in your entire body. He used to recite poetry to Isabella."

"No wonder she decamped," Adam said. "As I recall, Isabella eventually came to her senses and rejected Jim because their worlds were so far apart."

"I think she later regretted her decision. She may have married another man, but the marriage didn't sound much like a love match to me."

Adam shook his head. "Isabella wasn't the fanciful romantic." Pausing at the Fall River entrance to the national park, he paid the entrance fee. "You are. She was no doubt well aware Jim was bound to come to a bad end, as they say."

"He might not have if she hadn't left him," Sunny argued. "I read somewhere that, when he was killed in that gun battle a few months after Isabella left, he appeared to her in her hotel room in Switzerland. If that wasn't true love, I don't know what it was."

"Probably something she ate."

Leave it to Adam to reduce love to a culinary disaster.

CHAPTER EIGHT

"ISABELLA was torridly in love with Mountain Jim. She was not having hallucinations because she'd eaten mushrooms or some dumb thing." Isabella Bird had seemed such a sad and pathetic person to Sunny. Brave enough to strike out on her own and travel around the world, but afraid to risk love. Much like Adam. "I feel very, very sorry for your fiancée."

"You needn't. She doesn't care for poetry."

"I'll bet you don't even know."

"I know she wants to marry me," Adam said curtly. "And most assuredly she is neither secretly nor madly in love with me."

"How do you know? Obviously you know nothing about love."

"Sunny, I'm thirty-two years old and a criminal lawyer." Exasperation sharpened his voice. "I've observed more human behavior in and out of the courtroom than you will ever see. The entire range of human emotion has paraded in front of me, and believe me when I say the kind of love you're babbling about is an adolescent myth perpetuated by Hollywood.

"If you want your heart to pound, run up stairs. If you want trouble breathing, climb Longs Peak. But don't make the mistake of thinking either of those physical symptoms has anything to do with the relationship between a man and a woman. Liking, respect, common interests and similar goals are the foundation stones of a good marriage." He pulled into a large parking area.

134

"I'll bet you don't believe in fairies or Santa Claus or the Easter bunny, either."

"I'm certain you believe enough for both of us." His voice made it clear the subject was closed. "We're at Horseshoe Park, named for its shape. Long ago it was a lake formed by moraines."

Intent on their discussion, Sunny had paid no attention to the passing landscape. To give her time to muster up more convincing arguments, she glanced out the car window. Adam's stubborn denial of love was forgotten. "Elk!" she cried in delight. "Hundreds of them."

"It's fashionable now to call them by their Indian name, *wapiti*," Adam said. "Early settlers named these animals elk, but true elk are European. In the fall a good-sized herd comes out to feed in the meadow now, staying until morning." He rolled his car window down all the way. "Listen." The early evening air was filled with high-pitched mewing interwoven with loud clanking noises. "And watch that big fellow over there."

Sunny looked in the direction of Adam's pointing finger. Across the meadow a large bull with an enormous rack of antlers strutted through a group of cow elk and smaller bulls. The cows merely edged out of the bull's path while the smaller bulls darted away. A medium-size bull held his ground, and the larger elk halted and stared at the smaller and younger animal. The younger bull's courage lasted about a minute and then he, too, bounded away.

"Thought better of it," Adam said.

Sunny nodded, totally engrossed in the fascinating spectacle before her. From the meadow came a weird low bellow that ascended to a high scream before ending in a grunting sound. "That's the sound I heard from

the house last night, only louder. You said it was an elk
bugling. Which one is it?''

"Keep watching," Adam said.

One minute there was nothing but willow branches;
the next another set of enormous antlers emerged from
the heavy growth, followed by a bull's dark brown head
and lighter-colored body. The first bull watched the
second approach, staring intently. This time the arrogant stare failed to intimidate. The first bull lowered
his head, but the second came on. From the first came
that incredible sound. The second bull stopped to roar
back his challenge. Both bulls feinted with their antlers,
and then came together with an abrupt crashing of
antlers.

"Well," Sunny breathed weakly, "living in the city
one forgets how savage and basic nature can be."

"Survival of the fittest," Adam said. "The first bull
has gathered a harem and the second bull wants it. If
they can't fake each other out, they'll battle. To the
winner goes the harem. You'll notice the cows could care
less."

Getting out of the car, he came around to Sunny's
side and opened the door. "Maybe the bulls ought to
read poetry instead," he added dryly.

Sunny ignored the gibe. "What are all those smaller
bulls doing around the outside of the herd?" She followed him to the edge of the parking area.

"Practicing. They pretend to charge and then run off.
One day they'll be strong enough to challenge the big
bulls. Until then, they hang around hoping a cow will
wander their way."

Cars pulled up, spilling out people, most with cam-
eras on tripods. More elk wandered down the pine-
covered slopes, emerging from the willows to flow into
Horseshoe Park for their nightly browsing. Oblivious to

the spectators, the large bulls bugled their stirring challenges across the park.

Sunny shivered in the rapidly cooling air as the sun dipped below the mountains and shadows encroached upon the meadow. Adam pulled her to stand in front of him and loosely draped his arms around her waist. She stiffened, but realized almost instantly his gesture was nothing more than a simple means of shielding her from the evening chill. And there was no denying his warmth was welcome.

Through her jacket she could feel the strength in his arms. Erratic breezes mingled the aroma of pine and cool mountain air with Adam's masculine scent. His chin rested on her head while his breath sent a loose wisp of hair dancing against her cheek. She closed her eyes and surrendered to the hedonistic pleasure of being held and warmed and protected.

Around her people talked and laughed, car doors slammed, elk mewed and rattled antlers, and the fanciful notion stole over Sunny that melting into Adam's body would keep her safe. Where once his sheer size had been intimidating, now she welcomed the solid strength. Dependable. The word popped into her mind. Adam was a man a person, a woman, could depend on.

An electrifying bugle jolted her from her reverie, snapping her eyelids open. Directly in her line of sight two enormous bulls challenged each other for the rights to a harem. Sunny knew mating season had everything to do with nature renewing itself. Chemical urges drove the huge beasts. Sexual attraction, Sunny thought dazedly. This was what Adam had meant. The flagrant flaunting of masculinity, the primitive posturing, the lustful bellowing...

The growing darkness absorbed the bulls, and Sunny's imagination replaced the largest male with Adam. Substitute a loincloth for the psychedelic bikini, lengthen his hair, let the breeze caress his chest and kiss his nipples... Her fingers curled at her sides, and a second shiver passed through her body.

Adam's arms tightened. "We can leave if you're cold."

Sunny swallowed, clamping down on her too vivid imagination. "I wish I had my sketchbook," she said, steering her thoughts into safer areas. "You should have told me to bring it." The setting sun outlined the mountains in bright yellow. Deep shadows cloaked the entire park, and the elk slowly merged with the growing darkness.

"They're here every night. You can come back. This time I wanted you to hear it and feel it and experience it as well as see it." He dropped his arms and stepped away.

Abandoned to the cold evening, Sunny swiftly followed him to the car. "Did your brother bring Emily to see this?"

Adam shook his head. "She was barely two when he was killed. I didn't bring you because of the portrait. I've seen you sketching the birds and animals outside my windows, and I thought you'd enjoy seeing this. I was right, wasn't I?" Satisfaction laced his voice.

"Yes. Thank you." Fastening the seat belt, Sunny snuggled into her seat. Almost instantly the car heater spewed forth warm air, chasing the chill from her bones. They exited through a different park entrance. Houses lined the road, friendly light streaming from the few inhabited by permanent residents.

She studied Adam from beneath lowered lashes as he confidently drove, his hands resting easily on the steering wheel. His dark heavy jacket emphasized his broad shoulders and chest. The muscles smoothly curving beneath his skin she now knew were kept in trim with jogging and regular sessions with exercise equipment. According to Adam, long days in court demanded physical well-being.

Her lips curved upward. She could almost hear the fuss he'd make if she suggested they stop at a doughnut shop. Doughnuts were not his idea of a treat. No, she thought with sudden insight, Adam's idea of a treat was a father's portrait for a fatherless child. And elk, *wapiti*, for a children's artist who featured animals in her books.

"Tell me more about this Grumps of yours." Adam broke into her thoughts. "You don't seem to have the usual relationship between an older person and a younger one connected only by marriage."

"Martin calls us the original odd couple," Sunny admitted. "Maybe if I'd had other living grandparents... On the surface, Grumps and I don't seem to have much in common, but when Mom remarried, she and Martin were the proverbial newlyweds. They didn't mean to shut me out." She shrugged. "But you know how it is. Blythe was already married. And with Martin in the Air Force, we moved a lot. I suppose Grumps was lonely, too. We took to each other right away, and I guess you could say he's been my special rock in a changing world."

"Dillon said you lived with him."

"I have for the past couple of years. The rent went up on my apartment, which was already too small. Grumps lives in a big, old Victorian house, and his third floor was perfect for a studio, so it made sense for me to move in with him." She smiled slightly. "I fill the house with the smell of paint and he cooks."

"Doesn't living with an old man put a damper on your social life?"

"You don't know Grumps. All my friends adore him. As much for his far-reaching interests as his cooking. Last year he hired a college student to tutor him in

Spanish because he wanted to learn another language before he got too old. Not that he knows the meaning of the word old. He reads the latest books, goes to the latest movies, even occasionally listens to the latest music, to be, as he says, *au courant.*"

"How'd you get stuck taking care of him?"

"I didn't get stuck," she said indignantly. "Not only was I there, I was the best suited to help him out. Martin is stationed in Washington, D.C., now. He and Mom flew back and forth, and Mom came out for a week when I had the flu, but she hates being away from Martin. And Blythe does have a husband and four children."

"Who's caring for him while you're gone?"

"He's fine now, or I wouldn't be here. Actually, I wouldn't be in Colorado if Grumps hadn't insisted I come. He claimed I was making an invalid out of him, but the truth is he was concerned about my health so he hired a woman, Esther, to come in occasionally. He said he didn't need her, but he knew I'd worry if he was alone. He wanted to send me somewhere in the sun, but I'm not the sun-bathing type, so he badgered me into coming to Colorado and told me not to call, write or return until I quit looking like death warmed over."

"He must be quite a guy."

Sunny smiled, blinking away silly tears. "He pretends he's an old grouch, but he's really a sweetie. He hates people to know about his various charities. He tutors at a local high school and is involved with a number of organizations which help young people. They're our future, he always says. The most fun is when he lets me help him shop for toys for a local group at Christmas."

"I'd say he knows how to live."

"Yes." Digging in her jacket pocket for a tissue, Sunny blew her nose. "I'm sorry. I've been disgustingly weepy ever since I had the flu. But you're right. He has a unique gift for living, and I've been lucky in that he's shared that gift with me.''

A gift she'd been in danger of throwing away. Funny how clearly she saw that now. Thanks to Adam. The thought came to her that Grumps would like Adam. Stepping from the car in front of Adam's house, Sunny said softly, ''I guess I'm greedy, because I don't want him to ever die. I'd miss him too much.''

Adam unlocked his front door and stood back for her to enter. ''I know.'' He erased a tear from her cheek with a slow movement of his thumb. ''I'll be going along and suddenly it will hit me, no matter what happens the rest of my life, Chris won't be there. Each time, the pain is a stab in the heart. It never gets easier.'' After a second he added, ''But I think it would be worse if his death didn't hurt. Or if he'd never lived at all.''

Hearing the pain in his voice, Sunny turned her cheek into his palm. ''I don't care if death is a stupid life lesson or one of those dumb things that are supposed to make you stronger, losing someone you love stinks,'' she said fiercely.

''Yes.'' Adam enfolded her in his arms.

His jacket was cold and smooth beneath her cheek and smelled of Adam and outdoors. Finding comfort in Adam's arms was becoming a habit. A bad habit. His shoulder was already spoken for. Sniffing, Sunny stepped back. ''What a maudlin twosome we are. I'm probably suffering from doughnut deprivation. Those apples and raisins and birdseed you call breakfast are obviously softening my brain.''

Adam laughed and hung up his jacket. Reaching for hers, he asked, ''How about a real treat tonight? I'll order out for pizza. How does vegetarian with double sauce and no cheese sound?''

"Yucky. Get everything but anchovies and ask for double cheese."

"Well," Adam drew out the word. "On one condition..."

"I promise."

His eyes glinted with amusement. "You haven't even heard the condition. What if I said you had to sleep with me?"

"You wouldn't. You promised. Besides..." She laughed up at him. "You're afraid of Bud, David and Daniel, remember?"

For a moment he went very still, then he blinked and shook his head. "I wish people on the witness stand had your memory." Not looking at her, he leafed through the phone book. "The condition is you have to go to a party in Denver Saturday night with me."

"I can't do that," Sunny said in horror. "What about your fiancée? What would people think?"

"She's out of town, and no one would think anything except that I'm lucky to have an attractive date. The engagement is known only in our families so far."

Sunny shook her head. She couldn't go on a date with Adam. Not even an innocent one. A date meant dressing up, perfume, certain rituals, a blurring of the relationship. Business only, she reminded herself. The whole notion of a date held too many dangers. "You can go alone or take your sister-in-law. She'd probably enjoy an evening out."

"Joanna is in Belgium." Adam's jaw tightened. "Even if she could go, I wouldn't ask her. The party is an anniversary celebration for some friends. Their wedding date and hers and Christian's happen to be the same."

"Oh." The reason behind his invitation became clear. Obviously Adam felt obliged to attend for his friends. Just as obviously he didn't want to go. The realization dawned on her that the man she'd seen as above the weaknesses of lesser mortals wasn't quite as tough as he made himself out to be. A demanding Adam she could have ignored; it was more difficult to refuse an Adam who needed her. She gave it one last try. "I don't have anything to wear."

"Buy a new dress. And don't tell me you don't have enough money. I'll advance you some against the portrait." He hesitated. "Please."

Some people didn't play fair. "Order your stupid pizza." She glared at him. "With double cheese."

Adam unleashed a slow smile from across the room. "When you buy that new dress, be sure it's red."

The warmth in Adam's smile swirled around Sunny, heating her blood. She tamped down on the oddly exotic sensation uncoiling deep in the pit of her stomach and concentrated on Adam's remark.

"Red?"

"For the man you call Grumps. Red to celebrate how creatively and joyfully he lives his life."

Sunny stared at her image in the mirror in disbelief. Why had she listened to Adam? Surely one devastating smile wasn't enough to totally eradicate every grain of common sense she had. Sunny Taite was not the type to wear dresses that shouted "Look at me!" There was no doubt this dress shouted. Long sleeves were the only concession to modesty and the season. If the neckline plunged any lower, it would split the outrageously high hemline.

What could she have been thinking of? The fringe was at least twelve inches long and swayed and flashed and shimmered with every step. If her hair were shingled instead of falling in loose waves over her shoulders, she'd look as if she'd stepped from the pages of the 1920s.

The color of the dress was definitely red. Firecracker red or tomato red might be the color of joy, or even creativity, but this red was... She smoothed her hands down her hips, luxuriating in the lush coolness of the silk fabric. The color of passion.

Heat flooded her body and she turned away from the mirror. This was the dress she was stuck with wearing, so she may as well quit hiding in her room. Knuckles sounded a tattoo on her bedroom door. Taking a deep breath, Sunny yanked open the door and struck a pose. "What do you think?"

Adam whistled in appreciation. "Worth waiting for."

"Thank you, sir. You don't look so bad yourself." In truth, Adam looked absolutely gorgeous. Used to seeing him in casual clothes or business suits, she hadn't considered how sophisticated and impressive he'd appear in formal dress. The stark black and white evening clothes elegantly molded his athletic body. He radiated power and strength. And drop-dead sex appeal.

Forcing herself to ignore the dizzying flight of butterflies in her stomach, she giggled. Adam raised a questioning brow. "If you'd been dressed like that the first time I saw you, I'd never have mistaken you for a burglar."

"I might not have mistaken you for an intruder," he smiled lazily, "but I'm quite sure I'd still have kissed you."

The butterflies started to riot. Preceding Adam down the staircase, Sunny desperately chattered about every mundane subject she could bring to mind.

Through St. Vrain canyon, down the interstate past open fields with prairie dogs standing sentinel on their burrow mounds, under a V-shaped flight of Canada geese with their long necks stretched in front of them, and toward the brown haze hanging over Denver, she bounced from one frivolous topic to another. None dealt with the realization that lazy masculine sensuality was all the more dangerous when the male projecting it was totally unaware of its effect. Sunny was aware enough for both of them.

Fighting to block her awareness of Adam as male, it was some time before Sunny realized the closer they came to Denver, the more tense and withdrawn Adam became. She wished she dared smooth the slight furrows in his brow with her fingertips. Since she didn't, she redoubled her conversational efforts as Adam guided his car through downtown Denver's shadowed canyons.

Rush hour had peaked, but a steady stream of traffic still flowed along the major arteries. Adam snarled at a driver who abruptly cut him off. Realizing he was no longer listening to her, Sunny fell silent. His tenseness was contagious, and she looked down to see her fingers knotted in her lap.

Reaching the hotel was almost a relief. Sunny tossed her parka across the back of the seat before Adam locked the car in the hotel parking garage. Crossing the wide expanse of cement, her high heels clicked loudly in the echoing silence. Somewhere overhead in the garage a car engine roared. Adam jabbed the button for the elevator.

Attempting to ease his tension, Sunny said in a teasing voice, "I won't know anyone here, and if you abandon me, I'll flop on the floor and throw a tantrum. Be warned that red could stand for temper."

"Don't think that hasn't occurred to me," Adam muttered as the elevator car doors opened.

Two pretty teenagers were already inside. The girls' eyes widened as they took in Adam. Young shoulders straightened and young breasts rose with innocent appeal. Ostensibly ignoring him, the girls chattered vivaciously in high-pitched voices, their conversation punctuated with giggles. Adam gave no sign of noticing. Seeing the aloof expression on his face, Sunny tucked her hand in his elbow as the elevator shuddered to a halt. The heavy doors slid open.

"Sort of a teenage female mating call," Sunny said as the elevator resumed its journey without them. At Adam's blank look she added kindly, "You'll understand when Emily is a teenager." Adam looked thoroughly confused as they walked into the ballroom. Tables were set up for dining at one end of the long room.

The first people Sunny saw were Dillon and Blythe. Her fingers dug into Adam's arm. "Adam, look," she said. "What are we going to do?"

Adam covered her hand with one of his large ones. "We're going to go over there like civilized people and say hello."

The total lack of surprise in Adam's voice gave him away. "You expected them to be here, didn't you?"

"Dillon told me they planned to attend."

"Blythe didn't know I was coming," Sunny said through clenched teeth. The stunned look on her sister's face was evidence enough. "You and Dillon rigged this up. I'm leaving."

Adam imprisoned her right hand between his rigid arm and side. His right hand squeezed hers. "No, you're not. Life's too short for you and your sister to waste time feuding over something so trivial."

"It's not trivial when your sister makes raging accusations," Sunny hissed.

"I didn't know you were going to be here," she said belligerently to Blythe as Adam stopped in front of the Reeces.

"I wasn't expecting you, either," Blythe said coolly. "I suppose this was Dillon's idea."

It was obvious Blythe was still angry, and Sunny was darned if she'd let her sister think she'd come groveling. "It certainly wasn't mine." She glowered at the man standing beside her sister.

Dillon twinkled back at Sunny before pulling her into a huge bear hug. "Give me a proper hello. What's the point in having a sexy sister-in-law if you don't get to hug her and make a room full of men jealous?"

It was impossible to stay angry with Dillon. Sunny smiled tremulously at him. "It's good to see you." She turned her smile into a frown. "Even if you did play a dirty trick on me."

"Not me, kiddo. Blame Traherne. It was his idea. And one I was happy to go along with. Can't have my two favorite ladies fighting. Not to mention, ever since your little spat, Blythe's been about as easy to get along with as a molting rattlesnake." He gave his wife a level look. "Anything you want to add?"

"About what? Her indecent dress?" Blythe gave a high, artificial laugh. "At least it's more than *he* was wearing the last time I saw them."

"That's it," Sunny said angrily. "I'm out of here. Adam, I'll be in the hotel coffee shop when you're ready to go. Back," she spat, "to the house where we're living together since my own sister threw me out of her house." Sunny spun around to leave. Two things stopped her. Adam's painful grip on her arm and her sister's low cry.

"No." Blythe took a deep breath. "Stay. Please. I might have been wrong—"

"Blythe," her husband gently interjected.

"All right. I was wrong and I lost my temper." Blythe's mouth wobbled. "I know it's no excuse, but I've been so worried about you. You weren't bouncing back after your flu."

"And I overreacted," Sunny admitted, blinking suddenly damp eyes. "I've been so tired and depressed, and then when a project came along that interested me—"

"I showed up and acted like a big sister," Blythe finished, wiping her eyes on the linen square Dillon handed her.

"You are my older sister, and the best ever." Sunny took the handkerchief Adam held out to her and blew her nose. "But that doesn't mean I'm willing to let you run my life, so if this Walter of yours is here, don't you dare throw him at me."

"He's not here. Besides, he's already engaged to be married. He never told me." Both men started laughing. "I don't know what's so funny," Blythe said defensively, "he would have been perfect for Sunny."

"Walter is very good at what he does," Dillon said, still laughing, "but that dress would scare the hell out of him."

"I can understand that," Blythe said tartly, back to her normal self. "The dress is certainly—"

"Red," Adam said evenly.

"Of course it's red, but Sunny—"

"Wore it in honor of her stepgrandfather."

"Since when is Nolan's favorite color red?"

"If it isn't," Adam said, "it should be."

"I think Sunny looks great," Dillon said. He wiggled his eyebrows at his wife. "Maybe if you're nice to her, she'll loan the dress to you sometime."

"Dillon Reece! Do you have any idea how I'd look in that dress?"

"Sexy as hell, and certainly not like the mother of three teenage boys."

Color rose in Blythe's face. "I look terrible in red."

"You wouldn't be in it long," her husband assured her. Blythe's pink cheeks turned scarlet as Dillon led her away to greet other friends.

"Feel better now?"

Sunny looked up at Adam's question. "Don't look so smug. That was a sneaky, underhanded trick. It would have served you right if Blythe had started screaming at you in public, accusing you of seducing her sister and one thousand and one other sins."

"I was willing to take that chance."

"Why?"

"I noticed how you asked about their mother every time Bud or one of the other boys phoned you. I know she hurt you," he said carefully. "People frequently fall back on anger to mask their real fears and worries. Your sister said you were ill and exhausted, which indicated to me she was worried about you. So I called Dillon."

"I dislike busybodies who always know what's best for other people," Sunny said grumpily. Being further in debt to Adam was not part of her plan. Even if her quarrel with Blythe had distressed her, Adam wasn't supposed to know that. Or do anything about it. "Next I'll be hearing you phoned my mother and Grumps." His face betrayed him. "You didn't! Who else did you discuss this with? Did you take out an ad in *The Denver Post*?"

"I thought, if Blythe had called them, your mom and Nolan might worry."

"They wouldn't have leapt to the same conclusion Blythe did. Besides, they realize I'm—"

"Twenty-five years old. I know."

"Well, I am." Indignant blue-gray eyes collided head-on with warm, smiling brown eyes.

Without warning the floor beneath Sunny seemed to tilt, and the ballroom sizzled with foreign and dangerous vibrations. Deep within her an unfamiliar sense of want and need uncoiled and spread. Food, she thought almost in a panic. I need food. Adam's gaze lowered to lock on her mouth, and Sunny licked suddenly dry lips. "I hope we eat soon," she said breathlessly. "I'm hungry."

One corner of Adam's mouth curved up one millimeter. His gaze never wavered. "So am I," he said softly, "so am I."

CHAPTER NINE

Hours later Adam switched on the overhead lights and shook his head in disbelief as Sunny waltzed across the gray-carpeted living room humming softly. "I thought you'd been ill. Where did all that stamina come from?"

"Sugar and fat. I finally got some real food tonight." Sunny twirled, the long red fringe of her dress flaring above her knees before she sprawled in an inelegant heap on Adam's sofa.

She gazed curiously around her at his Denver town house. "Very sophisticated." A witty black pinstripe draped most of the seating, the sole exception a modern, dark forest green and chrome chair which looked highly uncomfortable. A large black-and-white photographic landscape hung above a stark, burnished silver-colored metal fireplace.

"I assume your decorator had a theme. Let me guess. Young man about town?"

"Do I detect a hint of censure?" Adam asked absently, thumbing through the mail he'd carried in.

Since he didn't appear to be waiting for an answer, Sunny didn't bother to tell him she much preferred his vacation house in Estes Park. Kicking off her red high-heeled slippers, she stretched out on the sofa and wiggled her tired toes. Kicking back after a formal party was one of life's more luxurious pleasures. Even Adam had removed his jacket, tie and cummerbund and unbuttoned the top button of his shirt. None of which detracted one whit from his appeal.

Sunny studied him from beneath lowered lashes, attempting to analyze what it was about him that was so attractive. He certainly wasn't handsome. His skin fit too tightly over his facial bones for prettiness. His face wasn't so much formed as harshly carved by a master craftsman. One with a sense of humor, she thought, contemplating the dimple punctuating Adam's shadowy chin. He'd shaved before they'd left Estes, but she knew if she brushed her palm against his face she'd feel the scratch of stubby bristles.

He looked slightly rumpled and tough and hard-boiled and cynical. Like a man who didn't need people, who didn't care about people. In Adam's case, appearances were definitely deceiving. He might look like the gangster she'd mistaken him for when he'd caught her breaking into Blythe's mountain home, but in truth, he was a fond uncle so crazy about his niece he was willing to spend entirely too much for a portrait of her daddy.

Sunny recalled a party conversation she'd had with an older gentleman who'd explained to Sunny his being called "Senator" was merely a residue of an early political career. The man had spoken in glowing praise of Adam making time in the midst of a thriving criminal law practice to defend those not always able to pay. "The patron saint of lost souls," he'd said with a chuckle. Not that Adam was a sucker, the man had quickly added.

Sunny wasn't surprised to hear Adam was held in high esteem and well liked by his friends and colleagues. What had surprised her was how pleased his friends were to meet her. Adam had hardly exaggerated when he'd said his engagement was not yet known. The CIA would be proud of how tightly that secret was being kept.

Adam tossed aside the mail and looked across the room at Sunny. "I've always thought this room needed something. Now I know what it was. A fairy-tale princess dressed in red.''

"If I'm the princess," she waved a languid hand, "who are you supposed to be? The wicked king or fiery dragon?''

He strolled toward her. "I was thinking more along the lines of your gallant knight. After all, I am the one who unlocked the magic tower and set you free for the evening.''

She gave him a severe frown as he towered above her. "You're an impudent knave to boast of tricking a princess. I should banish you from the royal kingdom.''

"Or reward me." Adam's eyes glittered down at her.

"For tricking me into coming?" She pouted extravagantly. "Next you'll say you want half my kingdom.''

"Half a kingdom is paltry." Adam lowered himself to sit beside her as she reclined on the sofa. "I demand a priceless treasure. One kiss." He slid an arm under the middle of her back. "Freely given.''

Breathing was suddenly difficult. "It's not freely given if you demand it," she said. Adam's gaze never left her face.

Sunny lowered her eyelids, but it was too late. Her heightened senses were aware of his breathing, his subtle yet masculine scent, the latent strength of his arm, the slick, silken sensation of her dress sliding over her skin, and most of all, of Adam's body radiating a warmth that surrounded and embraced her. She raised her hands to keep him at a distance. His starched white shirt was smooth against her palms, and she felt the rise and fall of his chest.

"I suppose—" her fingers crept upward to toy with his open collar "—I could spare one tiny little kiss." Leaning forward, she pressed a light kiss in the center of Adam's chin and then slowly dragged her mouth upward until she met his lips. Adam was still, his mouth warm but unresponsive. Sunny broke off her kiss, forcing herself to meet his gaze. "Satisfied?"

Adam gave her a lopsided smile. "Why couldn't you be Little Bo Peep with pigtails and a pink ruffled dress?"

"You told me to wear red."

"There's red." Adam outlined the deep neckline of her dress with a slow-moving finger. "And there's red."

Her skin was aflame where he'd touched her. She caught her breath as he retraced his route, this time slightly inside the edge of her neckline. "It's the color of joy," she whispered.

Adam shook his head, his hand sliding upward. "Not joy." His fingers encircled her throat; his palm barely touched her skin. "This red—" his hand closed around her chin "—is definitely the color of danger." He lowered his head.

From the time hours ago after dinner when Adam had led her onto the dance floor, Sunny knew she'd been waiting for this moment. His kisses were flavored with wine and coffee as he tasted her mouth. She clasped her arms around his neck and melted into the sofa, pulling him down with her. Adam's body was heavy and comforting. She slid her hands over his starch-slicked shirt and felt the sculptured strength of his muscles. His legs tangled with hers, the heavy fabric of his trousers whispering against her sheer nylon stockings. His scent eddied about her, enticingly masculine.

His kiss deepened, and Sunny dug her fingers into his shoulders. He broke off the kiss, leaving her murmuring in protest. The feel of stubble still registered on her skin.

Warm fingers pressed against her lips hushed her as Adam shifted his arm beneath her, elevating her shoulders. Her head drooped backward over his arm, exposing the vulnerable spot at the base of her throat.

He lightly caressed her chin before burying his hand in the loose waves of her hair. His searing mouth sought her beating pulse.

Electric current zinged through Sunny's body, bringing her both intense pleasure and aching need. Her fingers tightened convulsively and she drew herself closer to his body, frustrated by the fabric barriers between them. Adam trailed gentle kisses over to her ear and back to her mouth. Slowly and thoroughly he acquainted himself with the moist, pink flesh until Sunny was a boneless, quivering mass clinging to him.

Breaking off the kiss, Adam rolled to one side, in the process positioning her snugly between the back of the sofa and his hard body.

Sunny's eyes flickered open. Adam's dark-chocolate-fudge eyes were half closed, allowing a lazy, male gaze to roam possessively over her face. Sunny's toes practically curled at the warm sensuality he made no effort to disguise. "Are you through?" she asked breathlessly.

Adam smiled. "What do you think?" He curled a loose wave of hair around his finger. His gaze never left her face.

Sunny felt the color rising in her cheeks. Her stomach turned topsy-turvy as Adam shifted his weight, his hips scalding hers as his body came to rest closer to her.

"With the mail," she said desperately. "We stopped because you wanted to check your mail."

"I was wrong." He brushed a thumb very slowly across her bottom lip. "You're a scarlet witch, not a fairy-tale princess." His tongue replaced his thumb, bathing her mouth with warm moisture. "You've bewitched me, you know that, don't you?"

"No I don't, I didn't, I..." With a low moan, she gave herself up to his kiss.

When Adam finally raised his head, his eyes gleamed darkly with satisfaction. "Witch," he repeated softly, the word a faint puff of air against her heated cheeks.

Sunny buried her face against Adam's chest. She had no recollection of unbuttoning his shirt. Taking a deep breath that was filled with the male essence of him, she forced herself to call a halt to this delicious behavior. "Adam, we have to go."

"Go where?" he murmured. He'd slid her dress off one shoulder, enabling him to nibble along her sensitive collarbone. One of his hands rested lightly on her aching breast.

He had reduced her to mindless jelly and he still expected her to be able to think? Her mind cast urgently about for an answer. "Off the sofa," she blurted.

"You're right. We're a little old for this. Especially when there's a perfectly good bed in the next room."

Panic pushed aside heat and desire, and Sunny arched away from Adam, bringing her fists up to shove against his front. "No."

Adam smiled down at her, an indulgent smile, a smile that said one and a thousand things, most of them clearly saying he was prepared to be patient since his goal was not in doubt.

Sunny took a deep breath and concentrated on Adam's left ear. "I want to go back to Estes Park and sleep in my own bed. Alone."

He chuckled softly. "That's not what you want."

Gathering her courage, Sunny met his gaze. "Maybe it's not what I want, at least not at this moment. But it's what I ought to want, and what I'll be glad to have done tomorrow morning."

The look on Adam's face grew more indulgent. "I promise you, no regrets in the morning. In fact..." He played with the deep V of her dress. "Tomorrow's

Sunday. I can't think of anything I'd regret less than spending Sunday in bed with toast crumbs and the Sunday comics. And crumpled sheets.'' His hand curved around her breast. "I'm looking forward to a Sunny start to my day.'' His thumb found the tip of her breast. "In fact, I'm looking forward to a long, lazy, Sunny day.''

Sunny clamped her hand over his. The evening had abounded with intoxicating circumstances—a wedding anniversary, a celebration of love, romance in the air. Dancing and music. No wonder her equilibrium had gone totally askew, but it was time, past time, to call a halt to this dangerous activity. Her fingernails dug deeply into the back of Adam's hand. Easy enough to stop his actions, less easy to stop her body's memory. Her nipple seemed to rise, seeking the warmth of Adam's palm.

"I don't intend to share your bed,'' she gasped. "You're engaged to be married.''

"The wedding is over six months away.'' He tipped up her chin and sprinkled moist, warm kisses down her front, edging her dress out of the way as he went. "We'll be out of each other's blood by then,'' he added thickly.

His thumb was doing that business again. She was going down for the third and final time. With a last gathering of inner strength, Sunny shoved against Adam with all her might. He landed on the floor with a loud thud.

Laying there, he looked up at her. "You have a problem?''

"No.'' Sunny sat up and jerked her dress back into place. "I just don't want to sleep here. I'm not going to sleep with a man who's promised to someone else.''

Adam stretched out, his head propped on one arm, and smiled wickedly. "I wasn't planning on sleeping.''

Sunny rose and stepped quickly over his prone body. "If you want to spend the night here, go ahead. I'll call a cab to take me over to Blythe's house."

They were halfway to Estes Park, the low-slung sports car snarling its way through the dark, steep-sided canyon, before Adam spoke. "It wouldn't matter to her, you know," he said conversationally.

Sunny didn't have to ask to whom it wouldn't matter. "It ought to matter. If I were engaged, I'd scratch out the eyes of any woman who looked at my man, much less slept with him. And then I'd go after him with a skillet."

"You've already demonstrated your skills in that area," he said dryly. "Nor am I surprised to hear you endorse jealousy. Anyone who mindlessly believes in the juvenile notion of love is bound to think jealousy is something to boast of."

Sunny hugged her parka around her as they sped through the dark night. How ludicrous, and sad, that someone so caring denied the existence of love between a man and a woman. Perhaps, having passed the age of thirty without falling in love, Adam had convinced himself true love didn't exist. No doubt his courtroom experience strengthened his denial. He'd explained away his brother's passion by focusing on the common bonds between his brother and his brother's wife. Sunny wondered if Adam's future wife shared his empty philosophy. "Would you allow your fiancée the same opportunity to sleep around?"

"She's not interested in sleeping around."

"You sound very sure of that." She wished she could be as sure Adam wasn't headed for disaster. Impossible to convince him that one day he could fall deeply in love. Sunny prayed the woman he fell in love with happened to be his wife. "What happens after you're married? Do you intend to bed every woman who attracts you?''

"Marriage is a contract," Adam said evenly. "I have no intention of breaking that contract."

She believed him. Adam would never succumb to a love outside the bonds of marriage. His personal honor would doom him to a loveless life. She attempted to make him see reason. "You say that now, but if you're bedding every woman who takes your fancy before you're married, what makes you think after you're married, you'll be content with one woman just because she happens to be your wife?"

"I am not bedding every woman in sight," Adam said through gritted teeth. "Until you came along I've lived like a monk since the day I decided to get married."

Overhead two stars popped from behind clouds as the canyon widened. Sunny couldn't stop herself from asking. "Why me?"

"Ask me something I know," he retorted. "You're too short, you look like a teenager." He hesitated. "Except in that damned red dress. Your hair is plain brown, your mouth is always flapping, you're argumentative, and you rush into situations without thinking. Plus you're too damned naive and vulnerable." He added reluctantly, "You're talented and compassionate, with a huge capacity for caring for others, but you're totally wrong for me. Damn it, Sunny, you still believe in fairy tales."

The headlights of an oncoming car silhouetted Adam. Sunny could almost see the anger radiating from his stiff body. She smoothed red silk over her thighs. "Then wanting to sleep with me doesn't say much for your good sense, does it?"

"Damned right it doesn't. All I know is," he said half to himself, "every time I look at you, I want to tear off your clothes and see if the rest of your body is as impertinent as your mouth, as easy to ignite as your temper, and as soft as your head." He slowed the car as they rounded a sharp curve. "And as generous as your heart." The last words were barely a whisper, before he said in a loud, curt voice, "Now, shut up so I can concentrate on my driving."

Sunny shut her open mouth. Keeping her heart from singing out loud might prove more difficult. They glided around another curve, and a moon sliver smiled down on them from the narrow slice of visible sky.

If Adam Traherne wasn't in love with her, then she didn't know what love was. She almost asked him if he'd heard the bells. The ones in his apartment. She'd heard them pealing as clearly as if she'd been standing outside a church on Sunday morning. Joy surged warmly through her body. She wouldn't fight the truth anymore. She was in love with Adam Traherne. In love with a big, cranky, arrogant, hard-shelled, soft-hearted lug of a guy who didn't recognize love when, she giggled silently, it climbed in the window.

The thought of Adam's fiancée reared its ugly head. No, Sunny told herself resolutely, she wouldn't feel badly about a situation which was no one's fault. The woman would be better off with a man who loved her.

Sunny reflected on her decision not to sleep with Adam. If he thought one night or even one hundred nights would cleanse her from his blood, then it was time to show him the error of his thinking.

She smiled in the dark, taking a mental inventory of her supply of night wear. Not a stitch suitable for seducing hot-shot lawyers. Maybe it would be best to forget the worn nightshirt and ask Adam to aid her in unbuttoning her dress. By the time he finished, she suspected the lack of a sexy nightgown wouldn't matter to either of them. Her skin tingled at the thought. Crumbs in bed had never sounded very appealing, but it was strange how one's tastes could change.

Curling up against the door, Sunny took advantage of the dark to lovingly peruse Adam's profile. From this side, the dimple wasn't evident. She curled her tongue in her mouth, pure pleasure shooting through her at the thought of burying her tongue in that dimple. If Adam didn't strip her dress from her when he finished unbuttoning it, she'd turn in his arms and thank him with a kiss, managing to rub her body up against his, and then she'd taste his dimple. Her eyelids drifted shut.

One very provocative dimple was going to play a major role in her life from now on. Laughter bubbled along her veins. Somehow she didn't think Adam would appreciate knowing she'd fallen in love with his dimple before she'd fallen in love with him. Maybe she'd tell him she fell in love with his muscles.

An image which sent her thoughts in another scandalous direction. Adam would have to pose again in the bathing suit. Eventually of course, she'd explain the bathing suit hindered her creativity and would have to go. Of course, after that, not a whole lot of sketching was likely to be accomplished. Lost in her pleasantly erotic thoughts, Sunny blinked in bemusement as Adam switched off the powerful automobile engine. They were back in Estes Park, parked in his driveway.

"What the . . . ?"

Following the direction of Adam's gaze, Sunny saw the dark sedan parked beside them in the driveway. An uneasy premonition chilled her spine. Before Adam could insert his key, a woman opened the door.

Sunny had no trouble recognizing her. Even with eyes shadowed with weariness, Joanna Traherne was more beautiful in person than in her photographs. The artificial lights gilded Joanna's shoulder-length blond hair with gold and kissed her porcelain skin with warmth. An exquisitely elegant white robe, which Sunny suspected was cashmere, hung casually open to reveal equally elegant white silk pajamas. Pajamas which draped an elegant, willowy body and miles of elegant, long-limbed legs. Adam warmly embraced the elegant body.

Turning her eyes from the happy homecoming scene, Sunny pulled off her parka and hung it in the coat closet. She avoided looking in the adjacent hall mirror. She knew exactly how she looked. Short, rumpled, and anything but elegant. It didn't take a mirror to point out how drab brown hair could be.

Turning slowly, Sunny was immediately the recipient of a flashing, megawatt smile from the woman standing so close to Adam. How unfair that even Joanna's teeth were elegant. Sunny plastered an answering smile on her face. "Hi. You must be Joanna."

"And you're Sunny Taite. I can't tell you how excited I am to meet you. I wish Emily were older so she could appreciate this." Joanna made a comical face at Adam standing silently, his gaze steady on Sunny. "Can't you picture Emily at about age seven bragging to all her little friends that she has actually met Sunny Taite?" Joanna's eyes dewed. "When Adam told me..." Her mouth wobbled. "I'm so grateful. I'll never be able to thank you enough."

Joanna Traherne's voice was sultry, she was elegant and beautiful, obviously didn't lack for money, and Sunny wanted to take the tall blonde in her arms and comfort her. Sunny liked her, and immediately wondered why she didn't want to. "I haven't done anything yet," she said.

"I told Adam he could give me the portrait for a wedding present, but he said it's for Emily." Joanna turned down her mouth in a charming, exaggerated pout.

Adam had never so much as hinted Joanna was getting remarried. Her husband had only been dead about a year. Was this why Adam had been so skeptical about Joanna and Christian being in love? Joanna was smiling at her. Sunny had to say something. "I have a feeling Adam isn't given much to romantic gestures," she finally managed.

"Adam," Joanna said in a teasing voice. "Have you been boring Sunny with your blasphemous views on love?"

Adam draped an arm over Joanna's shoulders. "Don't worry. She doesn't give them a second thought. Sunny still believes in fairy tales and happy ever after."

Joanna's whole body seemed to slump, but almost instantly she straightened, as if hidden wires pulled her erect, and said brightly, "Sunny isn't an old fogy like you or I." She wrapped Sunny with a conspiratorial smile. "I tell Adam, by marrying him I'm saving some other poor woman from making the fatal mistake of falling in love with him."

Sunny's face felt as if it might crack around her smile. She'd known it, of course, from the minute she'd walked into the house and heard the way Joanna'd murmured "Adam" before stepping into his welcoming arms. If the embrace hadn't told Sunny the two were more than in-laws, then the warmth in Adam's brown eyes as he looked at Joanna would have.

Adam stood with his arm protectively wrapped around Joanna's shoulders, as if shielding her from something. Or someone. Hurt he'd think Sunny might tell of his kisses, she struggled to pull her thoughts together.

"I don't think, to save my own sister, I'd sacrifice to the extent of marrying Adam."

Confusion furrowed Joanna's brow at Sunny's acerbic voice, but before she could say anything, Adam smoothly interjected, "Don't mind Sunny. She's always cranky because I won't allow doughnuts in my house."

Joanna gave Sunny a commiserating smile. "He won't let me eat cheeseburgers." She patted Adam's cheek. "Europe was wonderful. All that lovely fat and cholesterol, and you not there to make me feel guilty when I indulged."

"Speaking of Europe, why did you cut your stay short?"

"I brought you a surprise," Joanna told him. "Your dad had to come back to Washington on business, so your mom and I decided to tag along." She turned her smile on Sunny. "Adam said you were staying at his vacation house for a few days while you worked, and I wanted to meet you before you left."

She looked back at Adam. "And your mom couldn't wait to see you, so here we are. Emily and your mom wanted to wait up, but jet lag won." Joanna bent her head to rub her cheek against his shoulder. "We had a wonderful time in Belgium, but I'm glad to be back."

Adam's arm dropped to curve firmly around Joanna's waist. It was time for Sunny to disappear. Bidding them good-night, she dragged herself up the stairs. Adam intended to marry Emily's mother. His brother's young and beautiful widow. Joanna was too lovely not to inspire love and devotion. How could Adam not love her? And if he didn't love Joanna, how could he be so cruel to her as to marry her?

Fifteen minutes later Sunny heard two sets of footsteps quietly ascending the staircase. Moving silently to the light switch, she plunged her bedroom in darkness.

Murmured conversation reached her ears, followed by silence. Sunny tiptoed to the bedroom door and cracked it open.

Adam was standing in the hallway in front of his bedroom door, his back to her. Sunny reached for her doorknob, then froze as Adam's bedroom door opened narrowly and Joanna slipped through. The elegant blonde handed Adam a pile of blankets and a pillow, nodded at something he said, and then smiled as Adam lowered his head to kiss her. It was a brief kiss, quickly over, and Joanna went back into Adam's room, closing the door behind her. Adam disappeared down the staircase.

Sunny gave Adam a few minutes before following him. From the bottom of the staircase she saw the sofa had been made into a bed. Moving silently across the room, she sat gingerly on the edge of the mattress. Adam's face was a pale oval in the dark room. He said nothing, but she sensed he was awake. "Why are you sleeping down here?" she whispered.

"Where else would I be? In your bed?"

Even pitched low, his voice managed to convey mockery. "I thought you'd sleep with Joanna," she said.

"With my mother in the house, and Emily and Joanna sharing my bed? And don't you think it's rather distasteful to start the evening attempting to bed one woman and to end it bedding another?"

"I think we ought to talk about that. Well, not exactly that." Sunny plunged ahead before she lost her courage. "About you and Joanna, did your brother's death bring you together, or—" she swallowed "—were you in love with her before?"

"I hope you outgrow this love fixation of yours," Adam said coolly.

"That's not an answer."

Adam heaved an exasperated sigh. "My brother died in the hospital a few hours after the wreck. He was conscious almost until the end." Adam spoke factually, without a hint of emotion. "The last thing he said was for me to take care of Joanna and Emily."

"He didn't mean marry Joanna," Sunny said, taken aback. Adam's explanation put a whole new complexion on things. It didn't bode well for Sunny Taite.

"He meant take care of them," Adam said, "by whatever means necessary. Joanna wasn't meant to be a single parent, and I'd think you'd be the first to admit a child needs a father."

"Everyone says you're a champion of the underprivileged and defenseless, but I doubt Joanna would appreciate her and Emily being lumped with the waifs of the world."

"You've seen Joanna. Does she look like a waif?"

Sunny smoothed the sheet near her leg. "How does she feel about you marrying her because your brother asked you to take care of her?" When Adam didn't reply, Sunny tried to read his face in the dark. "She doesn't know, does she?" Sunny guessed. "Adam, that's unfair to Joanna. If you feel obligated to marry her because of a promise to your brother, at least tell her. I'd hate it if I loved someone and discovered later he'd married me because he pitied me."

"I do not pity Joanna," Adam said in annoyance. "When I asked her to marry me, I pointed out the advantages of our union versus the disadvantages of her remaining single. Upon mature," he emphasized the word, "reflection, Joanna agreed with me."

"What you're planning isn't a marriage. It's a disaster. Marriages of convenience went out with the dinosaurs." Her fingers dug into the sofa mattress.

"Marriage has always been a merger between two people, each having something the other wants or needs."

"And what does Joanna have that you want?" Sunny challenged.

"Joanna is a lovely, gracious woman. She was a good wife to Christian and she'll be a good wife to me."

"And what does Joanna want?" Sunny wondered if the other woman hoped to live her life over with her husband's brother? A different idea Sunny wished she hadn't thought of forced itself on her. "Adam, have you ever considered that Joanna agreed to marry you because she cares for you?"

"Do you think I'd propose marriage if she despised me? I'm not a martyr to my brother's memory."

"I don't mean that kind of care. Suppose Joanna is in love with you and thinks you're in love with her?"

"Fairy tales belong between the pages of a book, not in real life. Joanna is marrying me because it suits her to do so. Kindly disabuse your mind of the idiotic notion that Joanna is a lovesick teenager. I have uttered no words of undying love nor has she expected any."

"What if you're wrong?" Sunny persisted. "What if she is in love with you?"

"If Joanna needs to pretend she's in love with me in order to satisfy some feminine whim which dictates one only marries for love and not for sensible reasons, that's her business," Adam said curtly.

"How magnanimous. And disgustingly patronizing," Sunny hissed. "Indulging the little woman's whim." She thought about Joanna's white silk pajamas and about Joanna sleeping upstairs in Adam's bed with only her daughter for company. Twisting a section of sheet around her finger, she asked slowly, "You are planning to sleep with her, aren't you?" The idea was so hateful she couldn't keep from adding meanly, "Or are you worried she might compare you and your brother in bed?"

"What makes you think I'd come out on the losing end of any such comparisons?"

"Your brother loved Joanna. Love makes—" She wrapped more of the sheet around her fist. "You know, it better."

"I keep forgetting your vast experience with this delusion you call love," he mocked.

"I know enough to know you ought to find out if Joanna loves you before you marry her, and possibly make her unhappy the rest of her life."

"What would you have me do?" Adam asked in an irritated whisper. "Declare undying love and see what she says? Or carry her off to bed and make mad, passionate love to her to see if she—"

"It wouldn't be love. You don't believe in it."

"—passionately breathes my name at the appropriate time?"

"Is that what your other lady friends do?"

There was a long silence before Adam murmured provocatively, "If you're interested, I could arrange for you to find out."

CHAPTER TEN

ADAM yanked Sunny's arm, catching her off balance. She landed flat on her back on the sofa bed with Adam looming over her.

"I'm not interested," she said before Adam laid his mouth over hers. Her response made a lie of her words, her lips parting at a slight tug of his thumb. His kiss was deep and moist. And scorching. He tasted of peppermint toothpaste. She pressed her hands against his chest.

He was bare above a sheet covering him to his waist, and his skin warmed her sensitive palms. As curly chest hairs sprang to life beneath her hands, Sunny slowly wrapped one around her finger. The scent of his soap teased at her senses. Cupping her hips with his hands, Adam hauled her up against his body and methodically and thoroughly plundered her mouth. His rock-hard body scalded where it touched breasts, hips and thighs through her nightshirt.

Sunny wrapped her arms around Adam, taking pleasure in the feel of corded muscles flexing beneath her fingers. Every thrust of his tongue sent a burst of liquid flame through her veins. Teeth nipped at the soft insides of her bottom lip before his lips slid from hers. His teeth nibbling along her collarbone felt unbelievably erotic.

Her ancient nightshirt had long ago stretched out of shape, allowing Adam to easily slide it down one shoulder after he'd unbuttoned the few buttons at the neckline. The cold air barely kissed Sunny's uncovered breast before Adam's warm palm curved possessively over her. His mouth returned to hers, swallowing her gasp of pleasure as he stroked the tip of her breast into rigid need. Clinging to him, Sunny melted into a formless mass of sensory perceptions. When Adam finally dragged his mouth from hers, she sank bonelessly into the mattress.

"Damn it, what are you doing down here?" he asked in a hoarse whisper. He lay stiffly at her side not touching her.

Sunny could feel the heat from his body reaching out to her. She locked her fingers together to keep them from straying. "I wanted to talk," she whispered back.

"Then why the hell did you kiss me like that? Earlier, in Denver, you refused an invitation to share my bed. You have no business flinging yourself into my arms now."

"Flinging!" she repeated in an outraged whisper. "You attacked me. What was I supposed to do? Scream for help?"

Adam drew an exasperated breath. "I would have let you go if you'd asked. You weren't exactly fighting me off."

Impossible to argue with that statement. Adam Traherne may have instigated the kiss, but she had been an enthusiastic participant. What's more, if he reached for her again, she'd go willingly back into his arms. Not because her body trembled at the thought, but because she loved him. And loving him, she had to make one more attempt to make him see reason.

"No, I wasn't fighting you off," she admitted, "but I didn't ask you to kiss me, either. Your mother, your fiancée and your niece are upstairs. One of them could come down at any time. And still we... We did what we did. Doesn't that tell you anything?"

"It tells me you're a tease. You knew damned well I'd call a halt before things went too far."

"Of all the lamebrain... I wasn't teasing you."

"I suppose that wasn't your mouth eating mine, or your breast shoving into my hand, or your hips gyrating against mine. I didn't force you to do any of that."

Embarrassment flamed through her body, quickly followed by indignation. Some hot-shot lawyer he was. Too stupid to guess the truth. Coming back from Denver she'd been ready to offer herself to him on a silver platter. That made her the lamebrain. Sitting up, she tugged her nightshirt into place.

"If you had any kind of a love life, a short, brown-haired, mouthy nincompoop like me couldn't get you all hot and bothered. If you're going to get hot and bothered by anyone, it ought to be your fiancée, only she doesn't attract you that way, which ought to tell you something, but no, you've made up your mind what you're going to do, and there's no changing it, so you'll marry Joanna and make both of you absolutely miserable. I don't care if you ruin your life, but Joanna has had enough misery, and she doesn't deserve more; besides, you said yourself bedding one woman when you wanted to bed another was distasteful, and marriage won't change that." She stopped to breathe.

Adam's low laugh mocked her earnest speech. "You needn't worry. Once Joanna and I are married, and she's in my bed, believe me, my thoughts won't be on you."

"Your wedding is over seven months away. You're not exactly an impetuous bridegroom."

"Joanna isn't the type of woman a man tumbles on the sofa. She's the kind a man is willing to wait for. Meanwhile..." He shrugged.

The insult registered. "You mean," Sunny said slowly, "I'm a substitute for Joanna." She worked it out aloud.

"You're not marrying her because of some nebulous promise given to your brother. That's an excuse. You're in love with her. You haven't taken her to bed because you're afraid to, afraid if you push her too hard, she'll change her mind about marrying you."

Instinct told her there was more. "Or maybe you've loved Joanna for a long time. You envied your brother, and now you've won Joanna, you feel guilty and disloyal toward Christian. Denying your true feelings is your subconscious way of dealing with the conflict. Even with your brother dead, everything in you shies away from bedding his wife. That's why you haven't slept with Joanna. You've won the golden apple, but guilt won't allow you to bite into it."

"If I ever doubted you had an active imagination, I was wrong. I'm fond of Joanna. I always have been. Don't read any more into the situation than what I've told you. I promised Christian I'd take care of his wife, and I intend to keep that promise."

"And what about tonight? What about trying to get me into your bed in Denver?"

"Erase the injured outrage from your voice. I told you from the beginning the attraction between us was purely physical."

"I thought you were starting to care for me." Blood pulsed painfully in her tightly clenched hands. "But I was fooling myself, wasn't I? The senator called you the 'patron saint of lost souls.' I was another lost soul, wasn't I?" Sunny paused to allow him to deny her accusation. He said nothing. "You didn't want a portrait. You wanted to rescue me."

"Sunny." He stopped.

Argue with me, she raged silently. Tell me I'm wrong. "I'm sure Dillon knows your reputation. He probably told you all about his pathetic sister-in-law who can't get her life back together." She hated the way her voice shook. "Was sleeping with me supposed to be some type of shock therapy?"

There was a marked pause before Adam spoke. "I'm sorry. I never intended to hurt you."

The self-reproach in his voice destroyed any hope she might have had. Honesty forced her to admit he'd never made any promises to her. Her own traitorous imagination had built foolish air dreams. Knowing she was to blame heightened her anger and humiliation. "You haven't hurt me," she hissed, "just pulled the blinders from my eyes. I was beginning to think you were a real person, but you're nothing more than a single-minded automaton.

"You made a promise to your brother, and you intend to carry out that promise, your way, come hell or high water. Do you really think your brother wanted you to marry his wife and make you both miserable? That's not the Christian I saw in the photographs. That Christian loved his wife and daughter. He loved life." She rolled off the bed and glared down at Adam. "I wouldn't have liked your Christian one tiny bit. He'd be too much like you." She practically ran across the room.

Adam's cold voice stopped her at the base of the staircase. "Don't think you can use this as an excuse to wiggle out of painting Christian's portrait. We have an agreement. It may not be in writing, but it's legally binding. I won't have Joanna disappointed. You refuse to carry out your end of our agreement, and I promise you, I'll sue your idealistic fanny off. Is that clear?"

"Very clear." Sunny squeezed the wooden banister. It was a poor substitute for Adam Traherne's neck. "It's also very clear I should have listened more closely to my older sister. You are a rude, surly brute." She started up the stairs.

"Now that we understand each other, I see no reason for our little unpleasantness to affect the rest of the family. They're still on European time so they'll be up early. I told Joanna we'd drive into the park to see the elk. You're welcome to join us." His voice was impersonal. The evening, the kisses, the conversation might never have taken place.

"I'll be sleeping in." Her bags could be packed in seconds.

Ten minutes after Adam's car disappeared down Bull Elk Road the following morning, Sunny was in her car. Viewed from the highway, Longs Peak, with its lid of snow, was cold and forbidding. A tear traced a warm path down her cheek. Adam had warned her about believing in fairy tales, but she'd remained a dyed-in-the-wool romantic who stupidly and naively believed in happy endings.

Fresh tears cascaded down her face. Darn it, she still believed in happy endings. Just not for her. What a fool she'd been. Actually believing Adam loved her but simply didn't realize it. Oh, yes, mature, worldly Sunny Taite planned to teach him how to love. She'd stupidly believed she could fight Adam's fiancée for his love. Love. Adam knew nothing of love. Poor Joanna. She'd already lost so much; she didn't deserve being stuck with Adam Traherne the rest of her life. Stubborn, arrogant Adam Traherne. He was making a huge mistake and was either too stupid or too bull-headed to admit it.

An image of blond, elegant, beautiful Joanna popped into Sunny's mind, prompting bitter laughter, laden with tears. Who was she kidding? No man engaged to marry Joanna could possibly be attracted to short, mousy-haired Sunny Taite. Adam Traherne had kissed Sunny as part of his mission to save her from drowning in her own wretched depression. Driving away from Estes Park,

Sunny knew exactly how Mountain Jim Nugent had felt when Isabella rejected him and his love.

The month of March was displaying its harsher side. A bone-chilling wind blowing all day from the direction of the Missouri River reminded Omahans winter had not yet loosed its grip on Nebraska. Squinting through the dark night and the cold, driving rain, Sunny wondered whose unfamiliar car was parked in front of their curb. The car hadn't been there when she'd left on a quick trip to the grocery store for milk and doughnuts. Neither she nor Grumps was expecting anyone. The car must belong to someone visiting one of their neighbors.

Blessing garage door openers, she pulled inside the garage and parked. Unfortunately, the garage wasn't attached to the house, so she'd have to dash quickly across the yard to the kitchen door or be drenched. She paused a moment in the small doorway at the side of the garage. Light shone from the dining room windows. Grumps hadn't pulled the blinds. Sunny could see through the dining room into the living room.

Grumps and a large man in a black topcoat stood in the middle of the room. Questioning her eyesight, Sunny closed the garage side door carefully behind her and crept over to the window. Adam Traherne stood in the middle of the living room, an airline bag slung over his shoulder. A black briefcase rested on the floor near his feet. Sunny hungrily devoured him with her eyes. Even from this distance she could see he needed a shave. Joy blazed through her body, a joy quickly extinguished by the memory of their last conversation.

What was Adam doing here? He'd been in Texas defending a woman charged with murder. The news on TV this evening said his client had been acquitted. Which didn't explain his presence in Grumps's house in Omaha.

Unless he'd come about the photographs. She'd halfway expected him to come charging after her when she'd run from Estes Park taking the photos with her. Not that his failure to follow her to Omaha had killed off any nonexistent, lingering hopes.

Why had he come now? She'd sent the finished portrait and the box of photos to Blythe, and Blythe had forwarded the portrait on to Joanna. Joanna had called, her voice so clogged with gratitude and tears, the only words Sunny had perfectly understood were "Thank you." Once again Sunny had been unable to dislike the woman who possessed the one thing Sunny wanted.

Had wanted. No more. Adam Traherne had never been the man for her. Patients always fell in love with their doctors, she reminded herself for the millionth and some time. Adam wasn't a doctor, and she wasn't his patient, but their relationship fit a familiar pattern. Adam had yanked her from her apathy, causing her to confuse gratitude and love. Any woman might. When kissed by a man like Adam.

Sunny shivered as the sharp wind pierced her jeans below her heavy down jacket. She couldn't cower out here in the rain all night, but going inside to make civilized conversation with Adam Traherne held no more appeal. Her life was perfectly happy and complete without him. Ducking beneath the window, she sneaked over to the back porch and set down the groceries to be retrieved later. There was more than one way into the house.

The tree had been planted decades earlier, and its limbs reached high into the sky. One stout branch arched across to the tiny deck clinging to the wall outside Sunny's third-floor studio. There was no door to the deck, but a screenless window provided access. She'd been on the deck earlier today filling the bird feeders hanging there.

Neglecting to lock the window was one of her bad habits. One she was thankful for now. Years of practice eased her way as she scrambled up the familiar, old tree and onto the deck. Stealthily she raised the window and lifted one leg into the room.

"We have to quit meeting like this." The amused voice came out of the darkness.

The studio flooded with light. Caught astraddle the narrow wooden sill, Sunny blinked her eyes into focus. Adam stood in the doorway on the other side of the room. He looked tired. Ruthlessly squashing an urge to fling herself into his arms, she demanded, "What are you doing here?"

"That's what you asked the last time I caught you climbing through a window. Don't you ever use doors?"

Sunny briefly closed her eyes to hide the pain. All she was to him was a source of amusement. "Go away."

"What's the big idea?" Grumps peered around Adam's broad back. "I saw your headlights when you drove up. When you didn't come in, and I heard a scratching noise, I said to Adam, 'Darned if she's not climbing up that tree.' It was all I could do to keep him from dashing outside, but I convinced him you were OK. Guess you should be, seeing as how you've been climbing that tree since you were a teenager."

Grumps scowled at Sunny over his eyeglasses. "But you ought to know better than to do it in the rain. You trying to get sick all over again? You're soaking wet. I suppose you had a good reason for sneaking in."

Sunny flashed him an exasperated look before throwing her other leg over the sill and stepping into the room. She looked at Adam. "What do you want?"

Adam strode across the room and moved her from in front of the window. "I was in Texas."

"I saw on TV." In chilly politeness, she added, "Congratulations."

"Anybody could have gotten her off." He closed the window, shutting out the cold, driving rain. "It was obvious she was innocent. The case was a political hot potato. The police were under pressure to solve it, and they moved too quickly in arresting his wife. His mistress did it."

Sunny moved to put some distance between her and Adam. "That doesn't tell me why you're here," she said stonily as Adam tossed his overcoat over her work stool. The dark charcoal suit he wore suited his large, strong, masculine body.

"I haven't paid you for the portrait."

"You could have mailed me a check."

"I could have." He loosened his tie. "Joanna said the photographs weren't with the portrait."

"I sent them to Blythe. Dillon is forwarding them to your office. Grumps could have told you that." She glared at the older man.

"He never asked." Grumps met her glare with a steady, unblinking gaze. "We were busy talking about other things. Your meager explanation about how Adam persuaded you to paint the portrait aroused my curiosity. I wanted to know a little more about him."

"What is there to know besides he's Adam Traherne, the patron saint of lost souls? That I'm one of many notches on his gun?"

Adam's mouth thinned. "How do you keep from strangling her, sir?"

"It's not always easy. The best thing is to ignore her when she gets her dander up. Course, sometimes that has a tendency to make her worse."

Adam nodded. "You wouldn't think a little pipsqueak like her could be so mouthy."

The two men grinned at each other in perfect harmony. Sunny barely refrained from grabbing the nearest paint pot and flinging it at both of them.

"If you gentlemen," she snapped, loading the word with sarcasm, "will excuse me, I'm going to take a hot shower. I'm quite sure the two of you will have a better visit without me. Seeing as how you're both interminable busybodies who can't mind their own business and who always think they know best what's best for everybody else."

She gave Adam a wrathful look. "Leave the check on my drafting table, and don't bother to hang around to say goodbye." She stomped from the studio, ignoring Adam's insufferable remark to Grumps about sparks flying off her hair. Her arm inside her bulky jacket burned where Adam had touched her when he'd moved her aside to close the window.

Fifteen minutes later Sunny wrenched off the hot water and stepped from the steamy shower stall. Hastily she dried off, wrapped a towel turban-style around her sopping hair, and shrugged into a scruffy old terrycloth bathrobe. After slathering lotion on her face, she crammed her glasses on her nose and dried some of the condensation from the mirror over her bathroom sink.

"How long do you think you can hide in here?" she asked the shiny face staring back at her. Darn it, she was through hiding and running. Ripping the towel from her head, she savagely attacked her hair with a comb.

How dare Adam Traherne harass her in her own house? If he'd wanted those photographs so badly, he'd have hot-footed it to Omaha long before this. He undoubtedly hadn't resolved his ambivalent feelings toward Joanna and, until he did, planned to meet his needs with Sunny. Did he really think months away from his scintillating presence and devastating masculinity would drive a wretchedly pathetic waif into his arms? Just because in the past she'd demonstrated her susceptibility to his male charms.

The bottom suddenly dropped from her stomach. What if Grumps showed him the painting? He wouldn't, she quickly assured herself. Grumps respected her privacy. Usually.

Footsteps sounded in the hall. Sunny cautiously pulled open the bathroom door an inch. Down the hall Grumps's bedroom door closed. He was going to bed. Adam Traherne had done exactly what she wanted him to do. He'd left. Never to return. The comb caught on a snarl in her hair, and Sunny yanked hard. Tears stung her eyes.

Finishing in the bathroom, she started down the hall toward her bedroom. From the floor above, a narrow band of yellow showed around her studio door. Grumps had neglected to turn off the light. With a sigh, Sunny climbed the stairs to the third floor. Reaching her hand around the wall to flip off the light switch, she caught sight of the tie which lay in a crumpled heap on an adjacent bookcase. The door slowly opened wide at her touch.

Adam stood motionless in front of her worktable, looking down at the watercolors and roughs scattered on the table's surface. Sunny's gaze immediately flew to the far right corner of the room. The painting leaned against the wall, safely facing inward. Her attention returned to Adam. His sleeves were partially rolled up, and even from the back she could see his collar was unbuttoned. A few more buttons undone would allow her to slide her palms up his chest . . . Anger flared. At him, at herself. She stalked into the room. "Why are you still here?"

Adam didn't turn around. "Nolan was tired and went to bed. He said to tell you good-night."

"You didn't need to stay to tell me that."

"He told me he's getting married next month." He kept his back to her. "What will you do?"

"Grumps and Esther asked me to stay here, but I decided to move into an apartment."

"I know how you feel about him."

The words were more question than statement. "His marriage won't change anything between us," Sunny said firmly. "I really like Esther, and they are so much in love—I think it's super."

Silence reigned for several minutes. Adam gestured down at her worktable. "This book you're working on..."

The odd tone in his voice immediately put Sunny on the defensive. "I suppose you don't approve. No doubt you think it's mawkish, sentimental slop. You're one of those machines who think the show must go on, keep a stiff upper lip and win one for what's-his-name. I'm sure you consider grief a complete waste of time. Did you even shed a tear when your brother died?"

Adam stiffened. "When my brother died, our parents were in Europe, and Joanna was distraught, plus she had a child to care for. All the funeral arrangements fell to me. And, of course, I was executor of Christian's estate." Muscles in the back of his neck tightened. "A person needs time to come to grips with losing a brother. I wanted that time. I wanted to wallow in my grief," he said heavily, "but Joanna and Emily were relying on me. I couldn't abandon them. I'd promised Christian."

Sunny opened her mouth, then clamped it shut. There was no point in renewing a futile argument. Adam either believed he was duty bound to marry Joanna, or he wanted to marry her and the promise to his brother gave him the rationale he needed. She wanted to feel anger and contempt. She felt sorrow.

Adam rubbed a hand along the back of his neck. "Joanna called me when she received the painting. She was crying so hard, the only words I understood were that what you'd painted wasn't a portrait of Christian. I was furious, certain you'd deliberately sabotaged the portrait to get back at me."

The harsh, unexpected accusation stunned Sunny. "I thought Joanna liked the portrait." How could she have misinterpreted Joanna's phone call so thoroughly? That Adam would believe her so mean and petty... A slap across the face would have been less painful. To think she'd almost fallen in love with a man who knew her so little. "Thank you so much for your fine opinion of me. As it happens, I keep my art and my personal life separate."

"I immediately realized you'd never stoop to vicious behavior. Joanna finally calmed down enough to explain what you'd painted was better than a portrait of Christian. You'd painted a portrait of Christian's love for Emily."

"Oh." A warm glow of artistic satisfaction edged aside the anger and hurt. She'd been successful in communicating her vision of Christian.

"This," Adam said, gently touching a painting, "is proof you don't, can't, separate your art and your personal life. With every word, every stroke of color, you've opened yourself to your readers. You're creating a very powerful, personal expression of grief. At the same time, the book will be one children like Emily will read for comfort again and again. Your words are simple, yet deeply moving, and the paintings are hauntingly beautiful." He turned an intense gaze on her. "You are blessed with a truly remarkable talent."

Adam's words should have pleased her. Instead they acted as leaden weights pressing her down. She didn't want praise or gratitude from this man. He'd harassed her, bullied her, and hurt her. And made her—tried to make her—fall in love with him. The look of pride on his face cut agonizingly deep. The look of a father watching his child, or a poor little waif, take her first wobbly footsteps. Sunny swallowed hard, fighting a painful rush of tears to her throat. She had to say something or burst out bawling. "Well," she said inadequately, "I'm glad Joanna likes the portrait."

"She does. She was afraid she was so emotional when she talked to you on the phone, you might have thought she didn't like it."

"No."

"She hopes you'll come to her wedding," he said abruptly.

"I can't. I'm busy." Sunny concentrated on Adam's dimple, as if that would make hearing about his wedding easier.

"You'd like Tony. He's fifty percent Irish and fifty percent Italian and one hundred percent crazy about Joanna."

"Who is Tony?" Sunny hated the pathetic thread of hope that crept into her voice. And her heart.

"The man Joanna's marrying next month. She was so overjoyed with Christian's portrait, she thought she might have forgotten to mention to you that there's been a slight change in bridegrooms. Tony's in. I'm out."

"I see." Joanna had jilted him and he'd come to Sunny for consolation.

"I thought you would," Adam said ruefully. "Christian would not thank me for marrying Joanna. Not when I was marrying her for all the wrong reasons. You were right about that, but I was convinced Joanna needed a husband to take care of her and Emily." He paused. "So I set out to find her one."

"You really are the most arrogant, interfering, busybody—"

Adam held up his hand to stem her flow of words. "I promised Christian I'd take care of his wife and child, and I had to do it my way. Candidate number one was a widowed judge. Two was a fellow lawyer. Then came a dentist, a rancher, no, the rancher came before the dentist. Next was a banker, then a stockbroker."

Adam thrust his fingers through his hair. "I was running out of suitable single men to introduce Joanna to. Then one day when she was taking Emily to the pediatrician for a check-up, a dog ran in front of her car in the medical building parking lot. Joanna swerved and hit Tony's new BMW, he's a heart surgeon with an office there, and the rest, as they say, is history. All I had to do was convince Joanna it was all right for her to be blissfully happy again, which, with help from my parents, her parents and Tony, I managed to do."

"I'm happy for Joanna." Had Adam come all this way merely to tell her Joanna was marrying someone else? The erratic pounding of her heart interfered with her breathing. And her thinking.

"I want to thank you for the portrait of Christian." He hesitated before continuing in a stilted voice, "I also want to apologize for my behavior. You may not believe this, but I never looked upon you as someone who needed saving. At first I considered you a nuisance. Then when I discovered who you were..." A dull flush stained his cheeks. "You were merely a means to an end, the end being Christian's portrait."

Sunny felt herself go pale. "It wasn't necessary for you to come tell me that in person." Tearing open old wounds was no kindness.

"I felt I owed you that much. I treated you as a passing aberration, a challenge to bed, a cute and sassy pipsqueak who stirred nothing more than my blood." He gave her a level gaze. "You have to know, if Tony hadn't arrived on the scene, if I hadn't found another way, I would have married Joanna. I had to honor my promise to my brother to take care of his family."

She could think of only one reason why Adam felt she had to know that. Hope buoyed her heart; fear of being wrong held her tongue. She waited for Adam to tell her he'd come for her. A long silence ensued. Her gaze dropped to fasten on one of the black, curly hairs visible in the V of his unbuttoned collar. The silence in the room seemed to swell until her eardrums throbbed with pain.

"Well, then," Adam said.

Her gaze flew to his face. The crooked smile on his lips failed to soften the dark intensity in his eyes.

"Thank you for allowing me to say my piece. As you requested, the check is on your table." Moving to stand in front of her, he lightly kissed her forehead. "Live happy, Sunny."

Live. The word assaulted her temples. Didn't he know she wanted to live with him at her side? Did he know anything about living and loving? He'd claimed he admired Grumps for knowing how to live, and he'd accused Sunny of being afraid to live. She glared at the rigid set of Adam's shoulders as he walked slowly away from her. Did he expect her to say the words? He'd rejected her once. Blast him and his stupid dimple. "Adam, wait."

He turned slowly, his face expressionless. "Yes?" he asked politely.

He'd been quick to hood them, but for one fraction of a second Sunny thought she'd glimpsed something in his eyes. Something that gave her hope. But what if she was wrong? What if she wasn't? "I want to show you something." She hurried across the room and spun the painting around. A millenium of agonized waiting passed while Adam stared across the room at the large water-color leaning against the wall.

Sunny twisted her fingers together, scarcely daring to breathe, knowing what he was seeing. A wide variety of trees and plants, wildflowers, birds and small animals formed an exotic border around a vivid woodland scene. Rugged, slashing mountains in the background sym-bolized strength and dependability.

At the center of the painting a large, magnificently naked man, accompanied by an enormous bull elk, stood, muscled arms akimbo, strong thighs planted wide, on the rock-strewn edge of a mountain lake. A strategi-cally placed branch preserved the viewer's modesty, although one sensed the man was totally unconcerned by his nudity. His entire concentration focused on the lake and a vague feminine shadow. A tendril of brown hair floated on the water and off the edge of the painting.

Sunny hoped Adam heard the birds calling and the wind sighing through the branches. She hoped he smelled the pines. She'd tried to capture the man at the exact second he caught sight of the bathing woman. The look on the man's face was heatedly sensual and full of the promise of love.

"That damned dimple has always been the bane of my existence," Adam finally said. "Don't you think you've made me look a little fat?"

That's all he had to say? The painting exposed her heart and soul, and all he could think about was body fat? "The only place you're fat is your head," she snapped, hiding behind a shield of anger, as if it were possible to hide that much hurt and disappointment.

"Not so fat-headed I don't know that Bear Lake is damned cold to be bathing in."

"And all those wildflowers don't grow there, and if they did, they wouldn't bloom at the same time. So what? If you want realism, take a photograph. This picture is a fantasy." In more ways than one, she thought bitterly.

He didn't look at her. "Does it have a title?"

"*The Stupid Fairy Tale*," she said flatly.

"If that brown hair floating on the water is yours—" Adam closed the studio door with slow deliberation "—the title should be *Love*." He moved across the floor to where she was standing.

At the look on his face, Sunny went weak at the knees. "Adam," she said lovingly. She wound her arms around his neck, parting her lips beneath his. For the tiniest fraction of a second, while still capable of rational thought, she regretted she was wearing her ratty, ancient bathrobe instead of red silk.

Adam didn't seem to mind.

Much later, he retied the heavy sash snugly around her waist. "That's enough of that, Ms. Taite. You may have forgotten Nolan is asleep downstairs, but I haven't." Smiling with deep masculine satisfaction at the color which flooded her face, he dropped a light kiss on the tip of her nose. "I don't know when I fell in love with you, but I figured it out seconds after I discovered you'd gone from Estes. I couldn't come after you, not until Joanna was taken care of." His voice deepened. "You told me once you'd love a man in spite of his flaws and imperfections. I know I have some failings..."

If she wasn't already crazy about him, the hint of diffidence in Adam's voice would have tumbled her headfirst into love. Her fingers entwined behind his neck, she met his warm gaze. "What about my imperfections? You prefer blondes—"

"Only in furniture."

"—with long legs—"

"Long legs are for moose."

"—and pouty mouths."

Adam's lips twitched. "I love you in spite of your flaws."

"I thought you didn't believe in love."

"I didn't. Until I met you." He pressed a quick kiss against her smiling mouth. "I've been hearing those damned bells of yours, so you'd better be planning to marry me. I won't take 'no' for an answer."

"You never do." She feigned an aggrieved look. "I should title the painting, *The Bully*. You're so pig-headed and set on getting your own way, I suppose if I said I wouldn't marry you, you'd bully, and badger and harass me until I gave in."

"No." Dark brown eyes glinted with hot, sexy laughter. "I know a much better way to persuade you." He lowered his head.

"You can't kiss me into agreeing to marry you!"

"Can't I?"

He could.

BRIDE'S BAY RESORT

UNLOCK THE DOOR TO GREAT ROMANCE AT BRIDE'S BAY RESORT

Join Harlequin's new across-the-lines series, set in an exclusive hotel on an island off the coast of South Carolina.

Seven of your favorite authors will bring you exciting stories about fascinating heroes and heroines discovering love at Bride's Bay Resort.

Look for these fabulous stories coming to a store near you beginning in January 1996.

Harlequin American Romance #613 in January
Matchmaking Baby by Cathy Gillen Thacker

Harlequin Presents #1794 in February
Indiscretions by Robyn Donald

Harlequin Intrigue #362 in March
Love and Lies by Dawn Stewardson

Harlequin Romance #3404 in April
Make Believe Engagement by Day Leclaire

Harlequin Temptation #588 in May
Stranger in the Night by Roseanne Williams

Harlequin Superromance #695 in June
Married to a Stranger by Connie Bennett

Harlequin Historicals #324 in July
Dulcie's Gift by Ruth Langan

Visit Bride's Bay Resort each month wherever Harlequin books are sold.

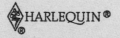

HARLEQUIN ®

BBAYG

HARLEQUIN®

Don't miss these Harlequin favorites by some of our most
distinguished authors!
And now, you can receive a discount by ordering two or more titles!

HT #25645	THREE GROOMS AND A WIFE by JoAnn Ross	$3.25 U.S./$3.75 CAN. ☐
HT #25648	JESSIE'S LAWMAN by Kristine Rolofson	$3.25 U.S.//$3.75 CAN. ☐
HP #11725	THE WRONG KIND OF WIFE by Roberta Leigh	$3.25 U.S./$3.75 CAN. ☐
HP #11755	TIGER EYES by Robyn Donald	$3.25 U.S./$3.75 CAN. ☐
HR #03362	THE BABY BUSINESS by Rebecca Winters	$2.99 U.S./$3.50 CAN. ☐
HR #03375	THE BABY CAPER by Emma Goldrick	$2.99 U.S./$3.50 CAN. ☐
HS #70638	THE SECRET YEARS by Margot Dalton	$3.75 U.S./$4.25 CAN. ☐
HS #70655	PEACEKEEPER by Marisa Carroll	$3.75 U.S./$4.25 CAN. ☐
HI #22280	MIDNIGHT RIDER by Laura Pender	$2.99 U.S./$3.50 CAN. ☐
HI #22235	BEAUTY VS THE BEAST by M.J. Rogers	$3.50 U.S./$3.99 CAN. ☐
HAR #16531	TEDDY BEAR HEIR by Elda Minger	$3.50 U.S./$3.99 CAN. ☐
HAR #16596	COUNTERFEIT HUSBAND by Linda Randall Wisdom	$3.50 U.S./$3.99 CAN. ☐
HH #28795	PIECES OF SKY by Marianne Willman	$3.99 U.S./$4.50 CAN. ☐
HH #28855	SWEET SURRENDER by Julie Tetel	$4.50 U.S./$4.99 CAN. ☐

(limited quantities available on certain titles)

	AMOUNT	$
DEDUCT:	**10% DISCOUNT FOR 2+ BOOKS**	$
ADD:	**POSTAGE & HANDLING**	$
	($1.00 for one book, 50¢ for each additional)	
	APPLICABLE TAXES**	$_____
	<u>**TOTAL PAYABLE**</u>	$_____
	(check or money order—please do not send cash)	

To order, complete this form and send it, along with a check or money order for the
total above, payable to Harlequin Books, to: **In the U.S.:** 3010 Walden Avenue,
P.O. Box 9047, Buffalo, NY 14269-9047; **In Canada:** P.O. Box 613, Fort Erie, Ontario,
L2A 5X3.

Name: _____
Address: _____ City: _____
State/Prov.: _____ Zip/Postal Code: _____

**New York residents remit applicable sales taxes.
  Canadian residents remit applicable GST and provincial taxes.

HBACK-AJ3

Bestselling authors

ELAINE COFFMAN
RUTH LANGAN

and

MARY McBRIDE

Together in one fabulous collection!

Available in June wherever Harlequin
books are sold.

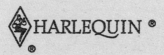

HARLEQUIN ®